SHOOTING STAR

As the captain pulled out several gold coins and bank notes and prepared to hand them over, Jessie heard a faint whisper of steel flying through the air. The man behind her let out a scream. Ki's *shuriken* had found its mark. The throwing star embedded itself firmly in the would-be thief's neck, just below the base of the skull. The sharp point of the steel star sent him to the ground in writhing pain, the gun dropping from his hand as he fell.

A second later, another whisper of steel cleaved the rain-heavy air, this one passing within an inch of Jessie's ear to bury itself in the silent thief's throat.

DON'T MISS THESE
ALL-ACTION WESTERN SERIES
FROM THE BERKLEY PUBLISHING GROUP

THE GUNSMITH by J. R. Roberts

Clint Adams was a legend among lawmen, outlaws, and ladies. They called him . . . the Gunsmith.

LONGARM by Tabor Evans

The popular long-running series about U.S. Deputy Marshal Long—his life, his loves, his fight for justice.

LONE STAR by Wesley Ellis

The blazing adventures of Jessica Starbuck and the martial arts master, Ki. Over eight million copies in print.

SLOCUM by Jake Logan

Today's longest-running action Western. John Slocum rides a deadly trail of hot blood and cold steel.

WESLEY ELLIS

LONE STAR

AND THE RIVER QUEEN

J

JOVE BOOKS, NEW YORK

LONE STAR AND THE RIVER QUEEN

A Jove Book / published by arrangement with
the author

PRINTING HISTORY
Jove edition / September 1994

ISBN: 0-515-11455-3

A JOVE BOOK®
Jove Books are published by The Berkley Publishing Group,
200 Madison Avenue, New York, New York 10016.
JOVE and the "J" design are trademarks
belonging to Jove Publications, Inc.

PRINTED IN THE UNITED STATES OF AMERICA

10 9 8 7 6 5 4 3 2 1

Dedicated to Gary Goldstein

LONE STAR

AND THE
RIVER QUEEN

Chapter 1

The lights of the hotel ballroom glowed warmly. The wallpaper was silk. The silverware was heavy. And the plates were rimmed with gold.

Jessie hated it. She sat in the ballroom of the St. Louis hotel thinking that she would rather be anywhere else. She would prefer to be hip-deep in mud, pulling a yearling out from the river, than at this hotel in St. Louis. But it was she who was stuck, not an errant yearling, and not in mud. She was stuck in this ballroom, stuck in a dress that was so impractical it had to come from France, and stuck at a table that featured the companionship of the most tedious sort.

"And then, quite abruptly, I might add, I just left," one of the women said. "I carried myself from there, away from that dreadful man, just as quickly as I could."

A few of the women and all of the men offered nods and grunts of approval.

"I cannot imagine what he must have thought," the woman continued, "but I can tell you well, very well indeed, what it was that I thought. And, I might add, I have never been so disgraced and humiliated in my entire life."

The small group nodded again in their well-considered approval.

"Do you not agree, Miss Starbuck?" a woman's voice asked politely.

Jessie, suddenly yanked from her thoughts, looked up to see that the entire table, nearly a dozen men and women, were waiting for her opinion. "Agree?" she asked, having only heard snatches of the conversation that had hummed around her for the past quarter of an hour.

"That I was correct in conducting myself as I did," the woman elaborated, her face a powdered mask of righteousness.

"I apologize. It has been a long trip," Jessie stammered. "I must ask, in what way exactly did you conduct yourself?"

The woman was taken aback, but pressed on, relentless. "Why, when the haberdasher, that presumptuous Mr. Teague, suggested that perhaps I was not suited to the bonnet I had selected."

Jessie studied the woman's face. She had a countenance graced with three chins and carried them so well that a fourth was joining. Her large, protruding eyes seemed to be held into their sockets only by the strength of the drooping eyelids. Diamond rings and heavy bracelets adorned both wrinkled hands.

"I think you were quite correct in leaving,"

2

Jessie said. "A hat isn't what you need at all."

The woman smiled. Jessie's opinion made her vindication at the table complete. "What do you, you people in Texas I mean, do with presumptuous shopkeepers?"

"Shoot 'em," Jessie answered quickly.

The women and men gasped, then seemed a little relieved at realizing it was merely a joke.

"Either shoot 'em or cut off their privates like pieces of rotten fruit," Jessie continued. "Mostly we just prefer shootin' 'em."

The table let out a collective gasp again, but before any of them could comment, a man in formal evening wear rose from the head table. The room silenced itself at his nod.

"My good, good friends," he began, his voice low and formal. "My good friends and business associates, distinguished guests and ladies."

The roomful of people shifted in their seats as the speech began.

"We are gathered here tonight for good companionship," the speaker continued.

"Hear! Hear!" someone at the other end of the room cried in approval.

"Good food and wine," the speechmaker intoned.

"Hear! Hear!" another voice shouted.

"And with good intentions," he added, "for we are here, as you all know, to pay tribute to a great lady."

"Hear! Hear!"

"And for all of you, friends, who have not had the privilege of meeting her, I would like to introduce you."

3

Two waiters in spotless linen jackets joined the orator at the head of the room. They labored under an enormous, velvet-covered load, like a huge board. When they were standing next to the speechmaker, they stopped.

"Gentlemen and ladies, may I introduce to you, the *River Queen!*" and with a grand flourish, he pulled the velvet from the painting to reveal a six-foot portrait of a river steamboat.

The room broke into thunderous applause, the entire crowd rising and yelling.

"May her reign on the river be a long one," the man in formal attire shouted above the applause. Then he added, "For she is the most elegant lady ever to grace the water."

As the speaker continued in his praise of the *River Queen*, an army of linen-jacketed waiters descended on the audience, filling their glasses with champagne. The entire process took no more than six minutes. Finally, when the speaker saw that every one of the two hundred or more people had their glasses filled, he lifted his own. "To the *River Queen!*" he shouted, holding the tulip-shaped glass aloft.

The entire audience stood, lifted their glasses, and drank.

As the revelers sat back down, the orator wound up his speech. "Gentlemen and ladies, the ship will depart at nine in the morning. I wish you all good sleep!"

With that, the people in the room began to disperse. The men wandered off to cards and billiards as the women bid each other good night and took to their rooms in the hotel. Jessie rose awkwardly in the confining dress she had purchased that afternoon and began a slow wobble out to the hotel's great hall, her feet unsteady in the French heels of her lace-up shoes.

As far as Jessie was concerned, the entire matter was pompous frivolity. She was only in St. Louis at the behest of one of her father's dearest friends, Richard Stempley, who was one of the investors in the ship. He had wanted her opinion of the venture. Stempley realized that Jessie knew next to nothing of ships, but he trusted her good judgment in all things.

Now, because she had performed a favor, or was about to perform one, she was trapped in a St. Louis hotel, in French heels, lassoed by a whalebone corset, and her long blond hair was stacked and piled higher than a longhorn's pride.

"Well, now, Jessie, did you enjoy dinner?" a familiar voice asked at Jessie's elbow.

"Very much," she answered, as she turned toward Stempley. She noticed now how much older he had grown in the past five or six years since she'd last seen him. The once great mane of red hair held more than just a little gray, and the sharp, blue eyes were a little duller.

Stempley shook his head at Jessie's answer. "I know my dear friend Alex didn't raise his daughter to be a liar," he said with mock disappointment.

"No, but he did try to teach some manners," Jessie said.

"Is castrating haberdashers a sample of those

5

manners?" Stempley asked again, smiling.

Jessie blushed, her pale features growing suddenly red and hot. "I'm sorry if—"

"Not at all, not at all, child," the older man said. "Ophelia and Owen Orwell are both of them pompous asses. Let me tell you a secret. She had all the money. Her father made it trading in Fort Benton. Owen is what she bought with it."

Jessie wasn't surprised. She said nothing.

"Just between you and me, I'd say she didn't get her money's worth," Stempley whispered in mock confidentiality.

Jessie couldn't help but laugh. The old man still had a bit of Texas mischief in him, even if he did live in St. Louis now.

"Have you had a chance to review those papers I gave you?" Stempley said suddenly, changing the subject.

"I have," Jessie answered quickly.

"And is she a good investment?"

"If those figures are correct," Jessie answered. "There might be a problem with the estimates per cord of wood. But what I don't understand is, why?"

"The estimates?" Stempley asked, playing dumb.

"Why the *River Queen*?" Jessie corrected. "It's a luxury boat. I don't understand the point of you investing in it."

"My investment was only in the lower deck, the freight," Stempley answered. "I can bring my grain downriver cheaper than any other way. Those freight offices were putting me in the poor-

6

house. For the next two years, I own those lower decks. Whatever vice they want to perform on the upper decks, that's fine with me."

"Then why bring me here?" Jessie asked.

"When I telegraphed, we were still negotiating my investment in the *River Queen*. Finally, they broke down to my price and that obliged me to invest. But in truth, I wanted to see Jessie Starbuck again. What has it been? How many years?"

"Too many," Jessie answered and gave him a hug.

"My dear, you shall start rumors and all manner of speculation that neither of us can afford," Stempley said as he moved away. He had made his fortune in Texas back in the old days and was not accustomed to displays of affection.

"Richard, I would wager that you could afford just about anything you took your mind to having," Jessie said, stepping back.

"That I probably could," he said. "But come, I'd like to introduce you to someone, I see him just now."

With that, the old man took Jessie's arm and escorted her across the hall. Jessie was still wobbly on the French heels of those damned lace-up shoes so it took a long time for the pair to successfully navigate through the crowds, pausing here and there to receive or give a word. Finally, after some time they were at the perimeter of a small knot of men.

Jessie, peering through to the center of the tight group, saw a man in a dark blue uniform. Nothing so gaudy as braid adorned the simple uniform, save for a half dozen brass buttons that ran up its center. But it was the man himself who held her attention. Well over six feet in height, he had a wavy length of blond hair just a shade darker than her own. The hair fell carelessly over his stiff collar, framing a face that included a strong chin, close-cropped beard, and the most piercing blue eyes that Jessie had ever seen.

"I understand, sir, that a competent captain can navigate in a foot of water," one of the men said, addressing the man in uniform.

"A good captain, yes," the uniformed man said. "I, on the other hand, require nothing more than a heavy dew."

"Thack, may I steal you away from your audience?" Stempley asked.

"Certainly," the captain answered, though his eyes focused directly on Jessie.

The other men, seeing that official business for the captain might be at hand, quickly made an opening through which he stepped. He walked with an air of utmost authority, moving through the men as if he assumed space would be made for him. He was, Jessie knew, a man who was well accustomed to getting his way, on the river as well as in the great hall of an overpriced hotel.

"Thackery Stratton, may I introduce you to Miss Jessica Starbuck," Stempley said. "Thack here is captain of the *River Queen*."

"A pleasure," the captain said, fixing Jessie with the stare of those blue, blue eyes.

Jessie leaned slightly forward as she reached out her hand, then toppled off balance because of her shoes. Before she could regain her footing, the captain stepped forward and caught her in his arms. Even through her dress she could feel the firm muscles packed beneath the tight uniform he wore. Yes, he was a fine figure of a man.

"Easy there," Captain Stratton said, bringing Jessie upright.

"It's these damned shoes," Jessie said by way of apology. "They're no good for anything except parading around like some crippled bird."

"That's what a good many of your sex do, I'm afraid," Stratton said slyly.

Jessie was about to refute the statement, but she could not. One look around the hall was all the evidence anyone would need to prove Stratton right. "However, is that not the way most of their men like women, crippled birds with pleasant plumage?" Jessie asked instead.

The captain seemed to think on this for a moment, then said, "So, tell me, Miss Starbuck, which is the bigger fool? Is it the woman who believes herself more beautiful for helplessness, because she confuses the two, or is it the man who believes the same?"

"For all I give a damn, they can both go to hell in a hurry," Jessie shot back.

Stratton let out a long, wonderful laugh then, all the time keeping Jessie fixed in his stare.

"Excellent! I knew you two would hit it off," Stempley said. "Excellent! Now, if you two young people will excuse me, I must take my leave. We have a long day tomorrow."

"Yes," Stratton said, then took Jessie's hand again. "I look forward to seeing you tomorrow, Miss Starbuck."

When Jessie finally reached her room, lace-up shoes in hand for the walk up the stairs, Ki was sitting up reading. His mixed Japanese and Caucasian features were sharply offset in the lamp's light.

"How did you find our friend Mr. Stempley?" he asked, setting his book down as he sat himself up in the divan.

"He's fine, Ki, he has barely aged," Jessie said, taking a seat across from him.

"That is good."

"He has already invested in the ship," Jessie said.

Ki, who had been with Jessie since childhood and was now her protector, raised an eyebrow in surprise. "He has purchased the ship?"

"Invested," Jessie corrected. "There are others, I believe."

"Ahh," Ki said. "And we are to leave tomorrow on this boat?"

"Ship," Jessie corrected. "Yes, we'll take it as far as Cairo, then take the train to Texas."

"Would it not be easier to stay on the ship until New Orleans?"

"Easier, but not any quicker," Jessie said. "Let's just get our hides back to the ranch. From my understanding, the *River Queen* ain't so much different than this hotel. And for my money, I'd

10

rather sit up for a week next to some damn drummer than spend time in a floating whorehouse."

"Yes, that is best," Ki answered after thinking a short time. "That is better."

"You could have come to the dinner tonight," Jessie said, stretching out her feet and wiggling her toes.

"Yes, I know," Ki answered simply.

"Then why didn't you?" Jessie asked.

"The entertainment is always better upstairs at the whorehouse than downstairs, regardless of circumstances," Ki said with a sly grin.

"You know something, I think you might just have a point there," Jessie said, then let out a long yawn.

★

Chapter 2

The next morning, directly after breakfast, they set out for the *River Queen*. A band was already set up at the docks, and as the first carriages arrived, the music began.

Jessie had to admit, the *River Queen* was a beautiful ship. The painting the night before had not done her justice. Every inch of the vessel was immaculate white. Gold trim outlined the first and second decks, and a pair of jet black stacks, rich with ornament, shot into the air. Jessie had seen sidewheelers before, many times, but she had never seen one so pristine. The ship was, she knew, built as a pleasure palace, with cargo only a secondary concern, but even she could feel herself falling under the ship's spell.

"It is very pretty," Ki said, as they stepped down from the carriage.

"A fine sight," Jessie said, making her way

through the crowd that had gathered to see the ship off.

The gangplank was covered with a thick red carpet, and it was bounded by a gold braid. Off to the side was another gangplank, the one that had been used earlier to load supplies and cargo.

Once inside, Jessie found the place to be a horror of gold trim, thick damask curtains, and silk wallpaper. It looked as close to a stylish hotel as anyone could come. The trouble Jessie had with it was that it wasn't a hotel. It was a ship. And everything, including ships, even luxury ships, should look like what they are.

As the steward showed them to their quarters, Jessie thought that at least she was comfortable. Gone was the dress and damned lace-up shoes. Replacing them were her favorite boots with a slight undershot heel, a pair of sturdy britches, and a blue shirt. Strapped around her waist was the double-action Colt .38 mounted on the .44 frame with the peachwood grips. Just feeling the familiar weight of the gun belt around her waist made her feel better.

They made their way through the main salon toward the rear, where the staterooms were located. Halfway through the salon, Jessie spotted Stratton. He was done up in a new uniform, this one with a touch of gold braid, and was surrounded by a gaggle of women. Just by the way they were talking, hell, by the way they were standing, Jessie could see how they were vying for the good captain's attention.

Jessie came to a stop and Ki paused right alongside, as the steward continued walking.

"It is a beautiful room," Ki said. Although he was aware of the object of Jessie's attention, he decided it was better not to comment. It wasn't that he didn't think the captain a fine figure of a man, but over the years he found that Jessie's amorous adventures were private. Though they shared many secrets, they did not betray the confidences of their lovers. This unspoken pact was welcome by Ki as well as Jessie.

"A beautiful room," Jessie repeated, then took note of her surroundings for the first time. The main salon was at the center of the ship. It was, she guessed, the largest of the ship's main-deck rooms. It was done up in polished woods and brass. Oil paintings of great ships and historic events lined the walls. The rear wall boasted a display of maps and nautical charts. Documents also joined the gallery, framed in thick wood and secured safely behind glass. A crystal chandelier hung from the center of the ceiling and thick Persian rugs adorned the floor. If Jessie did not know for a fact that she was on a ship, she might confuse her surroundings with the sitting room of some railroad or steel magnate.

Forward on the ship was the dining area, and just behind them the staterooms and smaller cabins. The deck above them, Jessie knew from the blueprints she had seen, was similar, with more staterooms to the rear, and a theater that graced the center portion, then a smaller gaming room with tables where men might pass the time over cards.

Below them were the cheapest cabins, crew quarters, cargo area, and kitchen. Far back in the ship were the boilers and stacks of cordwood needed to power the vessel.

This was not the usual arrangement for a steamboat, but then, the *River Queen* was no ordinary steamboat.

Captain Stratton, his eyes straying beyond his eager audience, took note of Jessie, then politely disentangled himself from their tedious mercies to stride with some authority across the room. "Ah, Miss Starbuck," he said in greeting, a sly grin playing over his face as he took in Jessie. "I see you have found more comfortable attire."

"Anything would be more comfortable than what I had on last night," Jessie said.

"And this is your servant?" Stratton asked, his attention turning to Ki.

"My companion," Jessie corrected. "And friend."

"My apologies, then," Stratton said, extending his hand. "Thackery Stratton, at your service."

Ki took the captain's hand, meeting the blue-eyed gaze head-on. He found nothing in either the captain's manner or eyes to suggest him to be a rogue or scoundrel. "Ki," Ki said simply.

"Well, Miss Starbuck, what do you think of her?" Stratton asked.

"Quite impressive, very impressive," Jessie answered.

"If you will excuse me, I will find my quarters," Ki said, and left without further hesitation.

Stratton nodded once in Ki's direction, then continued. "The finest ship on the river," he said.

15

"There's never been one like her, and I daresay there won't be one like her again. Not for a long time."

"Why is that?" Jessie asked. "Because of the rails?"

"In part. The railroads certainly can haul freight cheaper," Stratton said. "Rails were the worst thing for rivermen like me. But also because of the money. Men are becoming unwilling to venture their money on ships."

"I see," Jessie said, but really what she was seeing was little more than the captain's clear blue eyes.

"Do you know what bankers call ships?"

"I haven't a clue, Captain."

"A hole in the river into which you pour money," Stratton said. "Now that's a banker's thinking for you."

Jessie was about to say something, if not to defend bankers, then at least to dull the captain's verbal blade a bit, but before she could open her mouth, the captain was taking her by the arm and leading her over to a small group of men.

Before they were halfway across the room, she recognized one of the men as Stempley. He was done up in a pearl gray suit and silk hat befitting the occasion. The other five were dressed in a similar fashion.

"Jessie, my dear girl, please join us," Stempley said, a wide smile breaking out across his face. "I would like for you to meet my fellow investors in this little venture."

Jessie smiled politely, awaiting introductions.

"This, my dear girl, is Avery Strope, of the Kentucky Stropes," Stempley said.

Strope, a smallish man with a huge bald head and red nose, took Jessie's hand in his and gave it a courtly kiss. "A pleasure, my good lady," he said, fumes of liquor wafting from his mouth as if from an uncorked bottle.

Jessie pulled her hand back and offered a demure smile.

"And this is Nelson Seacrest," Stempley continued, gesturing slightly to a portly man, his suit coat stretched as tight as India rubber across an expanse of stomach.

Seacrest took Jessie's hand in his fat, pink fingers and attempted to lean forward to kiss it, as Strope had done. Unable to lean so far forward, he settled on raising her hand in his to his lips to perform the kiss. "A rare pleasure indeed," Seacrest said.

"Bradford Moran," Stempley pushed on, motioning to the next in line, a tall, thin man, younger than the rest, though not by much.

"Ahh, such a beautiful creature! What, may I ask, brings you to our vessel?" Moran said, then kissed Jessie's hand for longer than necessary. She could see then that he was the dandy of the group, the brocade vest, the abundance of jewelry. He was a vain man.

"Richard, of course," Jessie answered, finally choosing to withdraw her hand from Moran's. "When he sent word that he'd built himself a boat, I asked for a ride."

Stratton let out a laugh, then said, "Ship, Miss

Starbuck. The lady is a ship."

"And finally, this is Duncan Quigley," Stempley said.

Jessie offered her hand yet again and the last of the group took it in his and performed a small, perfunctory kiss. "A pleasure, dear lady," he said, with a voice tinged with a Western twang. He was leaner than the others, with a cooler and more polished manner. His face was neither soft nor bland, with pale green eyes. It was, Jessie assumed, a face that lent itself easily to the game of poker and the profession of finance.

Just then, a white-jacketed steward came up and whispered a few words in the captain's ear. He nodded crisply, then said, "If you'll excuse me, there is a small detail that requires my attention."

The other men nodded and in a flash the captain was gone, leaving Jessie with Stempley and his fellow investors.

"I take it, then, that you are the five responsible for the *River Queen?*" she asked.

"We five, and one," Stempley said. "Where in blazes is Delamore anyway?"

"Need you ask?" Quigley replied. "It would not be unkind to say that he's at this moment placing a wager on which of the two stacks will put forth the blackest smoke."

The others laughed at the quip, though not for long.

"That would be John Delamore," Stempley said. "Of the Cleveland Delamores. He is, as they say, a man with an infinite capacity for sport."

"For gambling; the man is a gambler, if I may be so unkind," Quigley said. "As a businessman, I have no use for gamblers."

"But is not business itself a form of gambling?" Jessie asked.

"Business, Miss Starbuck, is business," Quigley answered with authority. "Business is enterprise, hard work, and the application of one's intelligence. It is not the idle pursuit of pushing currency back and forth across a felt table. Business, in all its varied forms, is man's noblest endeavor."

"And the bucket shops?" Jessie asked.

"Ah, Miss Starbuck, what you call the 'bucket shops' are the temples of speculation. Speculation, Miss Starbuck, is the purest act of faith I know. Faith in the human enterprise."

"Filling an inside straight could be called an act of faith," Stempley offered. "I myself have prayed for just such an event many times."

"Kentucky whiskey is an act of faith," Strope offered.

"And French cuisine. I sir, believe in the French and their power in the kitchen," Seacrest said, though his tone was more than a little bemused. "I believe, in all due respect, that their genius is inspired."

Even Quigley could not help but smile at Seacrest's joke. "I would suspect, after further thought, that the matter is one of individual—"

"Taste?" Seacrest said.

"Precisely!" Quigley concluded.

It was then that Jessie noticed how the main salon had filled. It was now crowded with people engaged in pleasant conversation. More people crowded the rails outside. She was about to comment on it, when the ship whistles blew shrilly in two long bursts.

"We depart," Stempley said. "My dear, if you will allow me the honor of escorting you to the rail?"

Jessie answered by hooking her arm in Stempley's, and the group made its way outside to the rail, all of them moving in good spirits and in anticipation of the journey ahead.

Outside, the burly dock workers were releasing the lines that held the boat to the shore. Two more men were cranking the mechanism that raised the gangplank. Meanwhile, the band was playing to the great amusement and appreciation of the crowd that had gathered onshore.

The *River Queen* trembled slightly, then the huge sidewheels began to turn and they began to move away from the dock. As they progressed downriver, young boys and girls chased along the shore, waving and yelling. Their shouts were returned by the passengers lined up along the decks. Soon they were moving into the center of the river and the shouts of the children became faint and eventually faded away.

When they were well under way, the stewards began circulating, offering silver trays of champagne and delicacies to the passengers, who had collected in the main salon. Several toasts could be heard and much laughing. Jessie herself toasted the ship more than twice.

The journey had begun.

★

Chapter 3

That night, with the lamps glowing softly in the dining room, Jessie joined the captain, Strope, Seacrest, Moran, Quigley, Delamore, and Stempley at the head table. There were many toasts and many interruptions from the other passengers, but Jessie figured that without them, the dinner would have been hopelessly boring. If someone had set out to do it on purpose, they could not have found a stranger group, nor one whose members had less in common than those sitting at the head table.

As the ship steamed into the night, the stewards served dish after dish of exotic fare to all except Seacrest, who had brought with him his own chef to prepare meals to his taste.

Finally, after what seemed hours of pointless conversation, the stewards brought in the coffee. It was then, when the silver serving sets were wheeled in, that the captain rose from his seat.

"Gentlemen, Miss Starbuck, it's been truly a pleasure," Stratton said, obviously lying. Jessie had observed him through dinner and noted that the good-looking riverman was as bored as she was.

A few of the men made some sounds of hearing, but otherwise went back to their banter.

"I believe, now, the entertainment is about to begin," the captain said.

And as if on cue, a young woman, dressed in a fashionable dress, strode into the center of the room. Two stewards arranged before her a golden music stand, minutely adjusting it to her height, as another set the pages of music in front of her. When all was in order and the group in the dining room had silenced themselves, she began to sing in an operatic contralto.

Every occupant in the dining room stared, transfixed, pretending to enjoy the show. As the singer entered the second bar of music, the captain leaned close to Jessie's ear, so close she could feel his warm, moist breath, and said, "May I provide a tour of the vessel?"

Jessie rose quickly and silently by way of answer and they escaped the shrilling of the singer as they entered the salon. "Thank you," Jessie said, as the captain slid closed the doors behind them.

"And for what am I being thanked?" he asked.

Jessie, smiling, said, "For rescuing me from that caterwauling."

"But my dear," Stratton said in mock pomposity, "she is this season's diva."

"Sounds like a brood mare with last season's breech birth," Jessie shot back. "Now, about that tour, I've seen all of the ship, I believe."

"Have you seen the engine room?" Stratton asked.

"The engine room and the steam-powered saw to cut fuel wood," Jessie answered.

"Then you know ash and mulberry are the best fuel," Stratton answered slyly.

"I've always suspected so," Jessie said, taking a step toward the captain.

"And you realize that we burn thirty cords a day," Stratton said, himself taking a step forward toward Jessie.

"Thirty, you say?" Jessie said, smiling now, as she stepped forward again. They were less than three feet apart now and Jessie, caught in Stratton's steady gaze, could feel that strong sense of excitement. It felt like a buzz, right at her center. Like the vibrations of the ship's great engines coming up through the deck, but faster.

"Thirty cords, Miss Starbuck," Stratton said. "Imagine it."

"Not a tree is safe," Jessie answered, her voice a low whisper.

They were nearly touching now. Already she could feel something very much like his heat, feel his breathing and his heart, right through the three or four inches of space and layers of clothes that divided them.

"Not a tree, not a shrub, not a stick of timber," Stratton said, his voice as low as Jessie's.

"Imagine it," Jessie whispered, nearly breathless. Although they were only speaking, there was a thrill in it. This man made her feel like a schoolgirl with her first kiss new on her lips. She hoped she wasn't blushing, for with the thoughts that were running through her mind, she should be blushing crimson.

"I wager there's one part of the ship you haven't seen," Stratton said, moving imperceptibly closer.

"And what would that be, Captain Stratton?"

"The officers' quarters," he answered, his voice barely audible.

"The officers' quarters?"

"Specifically, Miss Starbuck, the captain's quarters," Stratton clarified.

"I would love to see the captain's quarters," she answered.

The captain's quarters were on the upper deck, just rear of the pilot house. As they made their way silently forward, they could still hear the high-pitched warbling coming from the dining room.

A low lamp lit the pilot house as the navigator stood stonily at the wheel. A large chart of the river lay spread out on a table to his left. Below, on the bow, a crewman marked the water with a line, calling out the readings as he pulled up the marked length of rope.

Stratton entered the small room first, Jessie hot on his heels. When he turned to click the small brass lock on the door, Jessie melted into his arms. With a deft movement, he secured the lock and held her.

Then he was kissing her, his warm, moist lips finding Jessie's in the darkened room. Their tongues played for a long time as he held her tight. Through her well-worn shirt, Jessie could feel the solid mass of his chest against her firm breasts. Her hands reached upward across his broad back, and she pulled him toward her. Even then, with the first kiss, she could feel his manhood hard and ready, nearly bursting through the uniform trousers and pushing against her.

Jessie wasted no time. She, too, was ready; she could feel it beneath the rough fabric of her own trousers. Breaking away from the kiss, she set her hands to busily unfastening the shining brass buttons of his uniform. When she had completed her task, she tugged it down over his shoulders, revealing the well-formed, masculine chest with just a dusting of fine light hair.

Jessie buried her head against the firm chest, inhaling that pungent masculine smell of sweat that was mixed with smoke from the engine room and the fresh aroma of newly cut wood.

Somehow, Jessie managed to pull herself away as he began to unfasten the buttons of her blouse. Soon, his strong, even hands were seeking out her firm breasts. His palms, lightly callused from years at the ship's wheel, brushed deliciously, teasingly, over her tight nipples.

Jessie shrugged out of her shirt, then hastily pulled the undergarment off, freeing her breasts.

The captain bowed his head as he bent forward to bury his face in her breasts. If it was ten, then it was ten thousand kisses he bestowed on her lovely silken breasts. Finally, when he reached their tingling tips, he teased her gently, taking first one, then the other between his soft lips.

Jessie melted back, her legs growing weak, and found herself reclining on his bed, a yielding and delicious platform of fresh down.

For just the briefest second, he abandoned her, and every inch of her body cried out for his touch. Then, when he joined her in bed, he was naked, his hard, well-muscled body next to her.

Slowly, he began to undress her, gracing each inch of flesh he exposed with the tenderest of kisses. From the smooth, graceful arc of her snowy white feet when he removed her boots, up and up to the tight underside of her calves, until finally he was planting kiss after kiss along the smooth, soft expanse of her inner thighs. His head moved easily from one to the other, his lips slow in their progress as she parted her legs, offering herself to him.

She thought she would scream out in trembling delight. Finally, when she thought she could stand it no longer, he was there, his lips gently teasing, pulling, and nuzzling in her silken thatch.

Reaching down, she ran her fingers through his hair, gently guiding him to her secret and most pleasurable places. Oh, how she wanted him, wanted him as she had wanted no other man.

When he finished teasing, he raised his head just a little, then began to kiss her soft heaving belly. Holding his head tight now, she pulled him upward, urging his progress.

With each inch of his forward motion, she could feel his manhood, hot and firm, first against her calf, then her thigh, until soon his head was once again between her breasts and his manhood was quivering against her moist and silken treasure.

"I want you now," she whispered breathily into his ear, her lips just brushing against the soft shell.

Then she reached down, and with one hand, guided him into her. Desire brought her hips high up off the bed as he filled her completely.

They lay motionless for a long time, enjoying the sensation. Jessie, raising her head just a little, kissed the line of his jaw, letting her lips trace a path across the closely cropped beard to his lips. They kissed once, briefly, and then he began to move.

At first he moved slowly, gradually drawing himself out of her until he was nearly completely free. Then, just as slowly, he came forward again, filling her with his manhood. He did this once, twice, three times, each time moving just a little faster, until finally he was progressing in smooth, regular strokes. With each stroke, Jessie rose up to meet him.

Soon their bodies were slick with sweat, and they were heaving and pulling against one another. Finally Jessie reached her trembling release, muffling a cry of pleasure against his chest. A second later, he found his release, every muscle in his body stiffening for just a moment before he began to slow the smooth, steady strokes.

They lay there, spent, in the narrow bed, each listening to the other's steady breathing, and sensing the boat churning and rocking slightly.

"You have lovely quarters, Captain Stratton," Jessie said at last. "Quite lovely."

"I am gratified you enjoyed a riverman's hospitality," Stratton answered, and then, with a half turn, he reached above the bed and groped on a narrow shelf of books and technical manuals until he found an ancient bottle of brandy.

"The glasses?" Jessie asked.

Stratton reached up to the shelf again, in pantomime, his hand searching for a pair of snifters he knew did not exist. "We could ring for a steward," he finally said.

"Yes, we could," Jessie answered, one finger idling playing along his chest, "or—"

"Or we could simply drink the brandy," he finished.

Jessie, bringing her hand up from his chest, took the bottle and leaned up on one elbow to open it. When she had the cork off, she tilted the bottle to Stratton's lips and he took a long, satisfying drink.

Jessie watched as he swallowed, then took a drink herself. The brandy was delicious, adding its warmth to the glow that already engulfed her. "A captain's life is not such a bad one, I suppose," she said after swallowing. She handed the bottle back to Stratton.

"It can be lonely," Stratton answered, then took another long pull from the bottle.

"Would you be offended if I called you a liar,

Captain Stratton?" Jessie asked, taking the bottle again for another drink.

"Miss Starbuck, it would be tantamount to mutiny," Stratton said.

"A passenger cannot be accused of mutiny, can she?"

"Miss Starbuck, as any captain knows, a passenger can be accused of anything," he answered. "And as every captain worth his salt knows, a passenger is probably guilty of everything."

"And what is the penalty for mutiny, Captain?"

"Nightly confinement to the captain's quarters," Stratton answered with a smile.

"Nightly? That doesn't seem particularly harsh, as punishments go."

"Did I say night? What I meant to say was confinement to captain's quarters several times a day, perhaps as many as three."

Jessie was about to say something, but before the words were out of her mouth, a bell began clanging, and the ship gave a mighty, shuddering groan.

Instantly, Stratton was out of bed, hurrying into his trousers. All expression of playfulness vanished from his face. Then the shouting began. Somewhere far off, a crewman began shouting, "Man overboard! Man overboard!"

There was no time to think. Jessie sprang from the bed and was into her pants and shirt, a second behind Stratton.

As they reached the main deck, they saw the crowd of fashionably dressed men and women gathered on the port side. Stratton, naked from

29

the waist up, spun a crewman around by main force and shouted, "Who? Who is it?"

"Mr. Quigley, sir," the crewman said. "He was leaning just here a moment ago, then I heard a splash and when I looked again, he was gone."

★

Chapter 4

By the time Jessie arrived at the rail, she found Stratton ordering a small group of crewmen to lower the small boats and hang lanterns over the side. As the boat drifted downriver, the crew continued to search frantically for Quigley, but to no avail.

Turning, Jessie spotted Ki, silently waiting and watching the failing rescue. As Jessie made her way over to Ki, other passengers in various manner of undress were joining the gathering at the rail.

"Mr. Quigley fell overboard," Jessie said as she approached Ki.

"Yes, I have heard," Ki answered, watching the men work. "How did it happen?"

"I don't know," Jessie said. "One of the crew said they heard him curse, then the splash. I suppose he might have tripped or slipped on the deck."

Ki looked down, as if he already knew what he'd see. "The deck is dry," he said at last. "It would be very difficult indeed to slip on a dry deck. And the rail is very high. He would have to trip very high indeed."

"What are you saying, Ki?" Jessie asked. "You think he jumped in to kill himself?"

"Perhaps that. Perhaps also, he was pushed."

Jessie was about to say something, but was suddenly interrupted by a voice at her elbow. "I'd call that the better proposition by far, Miss Starbuck. Man like Mr. Quigley, he'd be naturally reluctant to face his maker. Naturally reluctant and with damned good reason."

Turning her head, Jessie saw a tall man, no more than thirty-five, in a dapper gray suit. His lean face, unlike those of the other passengers, showed no hint of concern. "I don't believe I've had the pleasure," Jessie said.

"Givens, Miss Starbuck, Jerome Givens," the stranger said with a slight smile and even slighter nod. "Now, if you'd allow me the honor of purchasing for your refreshment a judicious quantity of brandy, before the others grow bored of the rescue and find they desire drink—"

"Mr. Givens, you don't seem to believe they'll find him," Jessie said.

"They won't, Miss Starbuck, not breathing at any rate," came the answer. "And if they do find the body, they'll find they require drink as well. Something about a drowned man, I have found, induces thirst."

"You seem expert on the matter," Jessie noted.

"Is that by profession or inclination?"

"A little of both, but not much of either, I suppose," Givens answered.

Jessie studied him, then said, "You give very vague answers. What exactly is your profession?"

"The same as my inclination," Givens began.

"He is a gambler," Ki broke in.

"Bravo, Ki," Givens said. "I am fortunate in that my profession and inclinations are identical."

"And your familiarity with drowned men?" Jessie asked.

Now it was Givens's turn to smile. "If you're going to question me, then it will be over a brandy or not at all."

With that, the three of them headed back into the empty saloon. At the far corner, a bar was set up, the bartender looking anxious as he stood alone in the room. A short time later, they were seated at a small table, two snifters between them. Ki did not choose to indulge.

"Now, what questions may I answer for you, Miss Starbuck?" Givens asked.

"To begin with, how did you come by this information about drowned men and such?"

Givens picked up his snifter and took a small sip before answering. "When you spend as much time as I do on ships, you come by a great deal of information. I have witnessed men jumping, slipping, and pushed off ships in lakes, rivers, and oceans. You would be surprised to learn how little difference there is between them."

"Those bodies of water?" Jessie asked.

33

Still holding his snifter, Givens offered a sly smile. "The end result, of course."

"And in your educated opinion, what was Quigley?" Jessie said. "Pushed or slipped?"

"Difficult to tell," Givens said. "The gentleman certainly had his share of enemies."

"Had? You seem awfully certain of his death."

"I would wager on it, I am that certain," Givens answered. "One of the things I have observed while traveling on those lakes, rivers, and oceans is that a drowning man will cry out for help—quite vigorously. A drowned man, however, is quite silent. That, Miss Starbuck is what I would deem a universal truth."

"And that man who is pushed?" Ki asked.

Givens took his time in answering. "I would suspect that would depend on how thorough the man who pushed him was in silencing him beforehand."

Just then, the doors to the decks opened and passengers began entering. They talked excitedly among themselves, and everyone headed directly toward the bar. Very soon a large group had gathered at the bar, with the bartender frantically serving drinks. It would seem that Mr. Givens had been correct in that assumption as well. He was, Jessie was certain, a man on whom the lessons of experience were not wasted.

"Shouldn't you be off, enticing the men into a game of faro or poker?" Jessie asked.

"On the first day of the voyage?" Givens asked in mock horror. "Never, Miss Starbuck, on the first day. Never."

"Bad luck?"

"There is no such thing as bad luck," Givens said. "But to put it in the words of my more notorious associates, they are not quite ripe yet."

Jessie took a drink of her brandy, then said, "Please continue."

"I said 'ripe,' but I meant bored," Givens said. "For those who watch ships pass, they are quite an exciting thing. There is a promise in them of distant lands and leisure. In reality, ships are quite tedious. There is little to occupy the mind or spirit."

Jessie, nearly blushing at the recent memory of the good captain Stratton, nodded for Givens to continue.

"There is the wholly satisfying conversation, such as this," he said. "Though remember, most people are incapable of intelligent conversation for extended periods of time. They exhaust their capacities quickly."

Jessie knew this to be true. Most people could talk about nothing but themselves.

"There is the promise of food," Givens continued. "But one cannot eat continually. Nor can one read or stand the constant din of entertainments such as we experienced tonight."

"The singer?" Jessie asked.

"Pleasant enough to behold, but very strenuous to listen to," Givens said.

"And then?" Jessie asked.

"And then, when they exhaust whatever meager resources they have at their disposal to fight off the lonely hours, I appear," Givens said.

"With a friendly little game of cards, I suppose," Jessie nearly sneered. She had always hated card sharks. She knew the type who drew the unsuspecting into a game, then slowly raised the wagers until all was lost on a single hand of cards. More often than not, they were cheats—nothing better than thieves, really.

Givens smiled a knowing smile, as if he could hear her thoughts. "Please, Miss Starbuck, do not insult me or your fellow passengers. Look around you. What do you see? These are men of finance and industry. Your fellow passengers are successful men. They are, in many instances, educated men. To offer them such a tawdry lie would be to insult them. In fact, I present myself truthfully and without reservation in relaying the truth."

"And they still play against you?"

"Play against me?" Givens asked, shocked. "In many cases it is they who initiate the game. If they desired an amateur, they could play at their clubs against their fellows. I merely offer them the opportunity to play against a professional in an honest game of chance of their choosing. As a professional, Miss Starbuck, I am an entertainment for them."

"For which they pay dearly, no doubt," Jessie said.

Ki, who had been silent for nearly all of the conversation, excused himself, satisfied that Jessie was in no immediate danger from this gambler.

Givens, nodding Ki good-bye, said, "Pay dearly they do."

"And you do not cheat them?"

36

"Cheating, Miss Starbuck, like stealing, is a refuge of the untalented, the uneducated, and the unintelligent. In gambling, cheating is the last resort of the loser."

"You do not cheat, yet you always win?" Jessie asked.

"Nobody always wins," Givens answered. "Not even the cheat always wins. But I win enough."

"By talent alone?"

"Yes, on the whole, by talent alone," Givens said. "Here, I will show you a trick of talent."

Jessie watched as the gambler withdrew from his pocket an ordinary deck of cards. He shuffled them twice, automatically, the cards working through his hands as easily as a well-oiled machine. Then, very quickly he divided the deck into three even piles on the small table between them.

"Now what?" Jessie asked.

"Now, if you were a betting woman—"

"Which I am not," Jessie said quickly.

Givens hesitated for a moment, then said, "If you were, I could offer to bet you that if you turned over the first card, it is either a jack, queen, or king. I would bet you ten tries at a hundred dollars a try."

"And you would lose," Jessie said, reasoning the answer out in her head, then counting on common sense.

"Would I?" Givens asked, then turned over the first card of the center deck. It was a queen.

"If you didn't cheat, then it's luck," Jessie said.

Quickly he gathered up the cards, shuffled them

again, and handed the deck to Jessie. "Try it yourself."

Jessie began to cut the deck into three stacks, thought again, and reshuffled the cards. When three piles were on the table, she turned over the first card on the left-hand pile. It was the jack.

Givens smiled, satisfied.

"I don't understand," Jessie said. "It doesn't make sense. A face card comes up every time?"

"Not every time. But enough times," Givens said. "It is a trick of numbers. The odds appear that the card will not be a face card. The odds would seem against you. But in fact, the odds are strongly in your favor. I could write out for you the formula, but it would be tedious. Be satisfied that it works and that is all you need to know."

"And people have bet on this game?"

"I have won hundreds of thousands of dollars playing this particular game," Givens said.

"Cheating, you mean?"

"It is not cheating," Givens insisted. "The deck is not tampered with and in many cases I do not cut the cards."

"But you know the trick."

"Knowledge is not cheating," Givens insisted, suddenly insulted. "Mathematical information is not dishonest. There are fifty-two cards and of those, twelve contain pictures on their surface. Those fifty-two cards are divided into three groups, containing approximately thirteen cards apiece. The wager is whether one of those groups, chosen at random, holds a picture card at the top. That is the wager. All of the numbers involved are known to all. Tell me, where in that does the dishonesty dwell? If you can tell me that, I will never play the game again."

"If it isn't exactly cheating, then it's right next door to it," Jessie said. "Now, if you'll excuse me, I must retire for the night."

Givens sprang to his feet to bid Jessie a good evening, and they parted company.

After leaving Jessie and the gambler, Ki was nearly to his room when he heard the crying. It was a low whimpering sound coming from a small closet in the hall.

Approaching the closet carefully, he listened intently, hearing the steady sobbing. It did not sound as if anyone was seriously injured, and he could hear no other voices, save that of the crying woman.

When he was close enough, Ki unlatched the small door and bent down to look inside. There, with her knees up nearly to her chin, was the singer.

With the light from the hall signaling her discovery, she immediately stopped. "What do you want?" she said, her lower lip quivering.

"Are you injured?" Ki asked. He could see now that she was wearing the same dress in which she had entertained the passengers.

"No, I'm fine," she said. "Now, just go on about your business."

"What are you doing in there?"

"I was crying, not that it's any business of yours," she said.

"You must come out," Ki said, offering the singer his hand. "It is not good to cry in a closet."

She didn't accept the hand. "Why?" she said.

"Why what?" Ki asked.

"Why isn't it good to cry in a closet?"

"Because it may appear foolish to those who do not understand," he said, still holding out his hand.

She thought about this for a second, then accepted the hand. It took her an awkward second, then she climbed back up out of the closet and began brushing her dress off as she rose. "And you understand, do you?"

"Yes, you wished to be alone, away from the passengers and crew," Ki said. "The closet was the first place you came upon."

"You do understand," she said, a little surprised.

"It is not hard to understand such things," Ki said.

"Well, you would be surprised how many people can't," she said.

"Many people do not wish to try," Ki answered.

"My name is Amelia Denton." She held out her hand.

Ki took the hand and shook it gently. "I am known as Ki."

"That's it? Ki?"

"Yes," Ki said. "Just Ki."

"Well, Ki, I suppose you know that they didn't much appreciate my singing tonight," Amelia said.

"Yes, I have heard," Ki said. "I did like it, very much."

The young woman studied Ki for a long time, trying to tell if he was lying to her. "You did?" she asked finally, brushing a wisp of reddish hair from her cheek.

"Yes, very much," Ki said. He seemed to see her now for the first time. She was a beautiful woman, the long red hair piled up on her head and the large gray eyes flashing, just a little red from crying. When she rose from the closet, he had seen the thin ankle and smooth line of her calf.

"Well, you must have been the only one," she said defiantly, as if challenging him.

"I cannot speak for the others," Ki said. "But I liked it very much."

"Well, I appreciate that, Ki," she answered.

He nodded, then said, "You should return to your room."

"What was all that commotion out there, anyway?"

"Mr. Quigley fell overboard," Ki said. "They are searching for him now."

"Did he drown?"

"It would appear so," Ki said. "I will take you to your room."

"Oh, poor Mr. Quigley!"

"I will take you back now," Ki said.

"No bother, it's just over here," she said. "Really, it's no bigger than that closet almost."

"Good night, then," Ki said.

Then, quite impulsively, she leaned across and kissed him on the cheek. "Good night," she answered, and hurried down the narrow corridor.

Chapter 5

Jessie awoke in the morning to find the ship anchored near shore not too far from where Quigley had fallen overboard. A small group of passengers wandered the decks, idly noting the efforts of the search party that walked along the shores and made their way up and down the river in small boats. As they headed in to breakfast, there was still no sign of the lost man. General conversation revolved around the fact that he was almost certainly dead.

Making her way to the dining room, Jessie took a seat next to Stempley and watched the linen-jacketed stewards serving coffee. The other investors were already at the table, as well as another man whom Jessie recognized as the ship's doctor. He was, at this closer inspection, a young fellow with dirty-blond hair and thin lips. He had the smooth, pale skin of someone who didn't get out in the sun much.

"Shame about old Quigley," Stempley said, taking a sip of coffee.

"Damn shame," Seacrest said, taking a large portion of sauce-covered something into his mouth.

"Hasn't seemed to hurt your appetite any," Strope asserted, taking another sip from a coffee cup that Jessie now saw held liquor the color of weak coffee.

"It would, except that Pierre is such a damn fine cook," Seacrest answered. "Finest Frenchie cook in the world."

"His name really isn't Pierre, is it?" Moran asked, sipping his coffee.

"Naw, I just call all Frenchie cooks Pierre; easier that way," Seacrest answered. "But this is the best one I've ever seen."

"The captain announced that they'll discontinue the search in a few hours," the doctor offered.

"Oh, Jessie, my apologies. I'd like you to meet Randolph Wittick the Third, no less," Stempley said.

Jessie nodded toward the doctor and gave him a small smile. "The third, no less," she said.

"Silly tradition, really," Wittick replied. "Some people, I suppose, place a great deal of stock in numbers."

"But not Randy here, right?" Strope said.

Jessie watched the faint expression of disapproval cross the doctor's face at the shortening of his name. She guessed that he, too, was one of those people who placed a great deal of stock in numbers and probably the title of doctor as well.

"I would speculate that the current carried the body downriver," Moran said. "No sense in waiting around here."

"Hell, ol' Quigley'll probably beat us to Cairo by half a day," Strope announced.

The men met this news with a burst of good-natured chuckling.

"I must say, none of you seem too upset about his apparent demise," Jessie said.

"Well, Jessie, you just didn't know him like we did," Stempley answered. "Old Quigley, he was pleasant enough to talk to now and again, but it's like they say, you really can't judge a man's character until you've done business with him."

"He had the character of a damned river rat," Strope said.

"Trust me when I declare that you have grievously insulted the rodents," Seacrest offered. "And no insult at all to Quigley."

"It is bad luck to speak ill of the dead," Wittick said.

"To speak badly is bad luck, Doctor," Seacrest chuckled, "but to speak can hardly be considered bad luck."

"Perhaps," the doctor agreed. "In any event, just now I find myself famished."

Jessie, already growing bored with the conversation, excused herself. As she began making her way to the bridge, a shudder ran through the ship and the two large wheels at the back began churning the water.

Apparently they had abandoned the search and were proceeding to Cairo, she thought to herself.

Still, it seemed a short time to search for a man as important as Quigley.

She found Stratton on the bridge, engaged at the wheel. His eyes were fixed on the river in the middle distance. He paid no mind to the three crewmen who went about their tasks in the small room, nor to Jessie, for that matter.

From up on the bridge, she noticed the river looked different. Here she could see the river, from bank to bank, and straight ahead to the gentle curve in the distance. The bridge greatly enhanced the expanse, making it seem more like a wide lake than a flowing body of water.

Jessie watched, fascinated, as they moved out into the center of the river, the wide boat meeting the gentle current as the wheels continued to labor behind them. The thing that especially held her attention was the captain. He appeared to stand just a little taller at the wheel. His hands, which had only hours before caressed her body, seemed even more knowing and familiar on the wheel.

Finally, one of the crewmen took notice of her, his eyes widening slightly in surprise. "Passenger on the bridge," he said clearly.

Stratton spun quickly around, but the mask of annoyance on his face quickly faded when he saw it was Jessie, and he flashed her a thin smile. "'Morning to you, Miss Starbuck," he said, turning his attention back to the river.

"Good morning," Jessie answered. "Though I am surprised we're moving on our way so quickly."

"Nothing to do," Stratton answered. "I've left two men behind to search the banks by boat, though I doubt they will find a trace of Quigley."

"Why is that?" Jessie asked. Her eyes were now glued to the river as well. There was something captivating in it that forced her attention to it, as if looking into a fire on a cold night.

"We were in the current when he fell over the side," Stratton said. "That current could have pulled him down, drawing him along the bottom like a carp. I've seen men vanish and not rise to the surface for miles."

"There certainly doesn't seem to be much mourning for him," Jessie said. "Particularly among his friends."

"Very tough man to mourn, Quigley," Stratton said. "They began well enough, those men, but as I understand it, they soon turned on one another. Business and friendship rarely mix well. I, myself, didn't know him well enough."

"In any event, when will we arrive in Cairo?" she asked, eyes still on the river.

"In time for a late supper," the captain answered. "Would you care to take the wheel?"

A few of the crewmen exchanged knowing glances, but Jessie paid them no mind, stepping forward next to Stratton at the large wheel of newly polished wood.

"Hold it here and here," Stratton said, showing Jessie how to position her hands.

Jessie took hold and felt the low-pitched vibration of the engine as well as the force of the current.

"Do you feel it?" Stratton asked, as if reading her mind.

"Yes," Jessie asked, fighting to control the wheel, which seemed to have a mind of its own.

"That's the river," Stratton answered. "She's talking to you through the wheel. Feel her."

Jessie loosened her grip on the wheel, letting it progress a quarter turn to the left. Slowly, the ship's course changed. "It isn't so hard as I expected," she said.

"On a day like today, no, it isn't," Stratton answered. "The sky is clear and the wind is mild. But on a day when the wind cuts across the river, now, that's a chore."

Fighting the wheel back into position, Jessie took up the original course. "Why is that?"

"The shallow draft," Stratton answered. "The wind catches the side of the ship like a sail, and because of the shallow draft there is no resistance in the water. I've seen boats pushed into the banks like toys. On days like that you have to fight for every inch to keep in the center of the water."

Jessie held the wheel for a long time, until she could feel her arms and shoulders becoming weary from the task. When she felt she could hold it no more, Stratton retook his position easily, standing so close that they nearly touched at the hips.

Ki made his way through the narrow hall with a plate of food. He had not seen the singer, Amelia, at breakfast, and he knew she would be hungry.

47

Perhaps it was shame that caused her to stay in her room, perhaps it was pride. In either case, she would still be hungry.

When he reached the door, he knocked lightly and a small voice within the room answered.

"It is Ki. I have brought you some food," he said to the closed door.

"Go away, Mr. Ki," Amelia answered. "I just ain't hungry."

"I will leave it here," Ki said, setting the tray down noisily. He then picked it up silently.

Something stirred on the other side of the door and a moment later, the door opened. Amelia stood there in the same clothes she wore the night before. Her eyes were red-rimmed from crying and lack of sleep. "I thought you were going to leave it." she said.

"I will hand it to you," Ki said, and handed her the tray.

"Well, you're here, might as well come in," she answered and stepped back into the tiny room.

Ki followed her in, setting the tray down on a small table, then taking a chair. Amelia sat on the bed. The room was so small that their knees nearly touched. The sound of the engine was loud and the vibrations strong in this part of the ship.

When Amelia removed the linen covering the plate, she found a large quantity of buttered cornbread, an apple, and some dried fruit. "I swear, I just don't think I could eat a thing," she said.

"You should try," Ki insisted.

"Well, I can try, I suppose," she said, tentatively tasting a piece of cornbread. "My, this is good, though."

Ki watched as she devoured everything on the plate, then looked up, her eyes wide and surprised at her own appetite. "I suppose I was just starving, after all," she said.

"Do you feel better?" Ki asked.

"As a matter of fact, I do," she answered. "Though I don't know how I'm going to face those people tonight."

"If I may suggest a way—" Ki said.

"Anything, though I don't see how it will help my singing," she replied.

"Perhaps it is not your singing, but the material."

"Opera, you mean?"

"Yes, these people, I have observed, do not like opera," Ki explained. "If you perhaps would try something more to their liking, then they would stay to listen to you."

"But rich people like opera," she said. "Every seat in the operas in New York are sold before—"

"Perhaps they like the purchase of the seat more than the music," Ki suggested. "Perhaps they appreciate not the music, but the fact that others may observe them in their appreciation of the music."

"That would explain a lot," Amelia said.

"Yes, it would," Ki answered, then rose to leave.

Amelia rose, too, and when they met at the door, they nearly collided. "Ki, I don't know how to thank you," she said. "I mean, for talking to me and bringing the food and all."

"There is no need to thank me," Ki answered.

"But maybe I can think of a way," she said, then brought her arms around Ki and offered him a full kiss on the mouth.

"There is no—" Ki began, but she quickly silenced him with a finger to his lips.

As he stood there, the young woman suddenly drew herself down to her knees. Then, kneeling in front of Ki, she gently worked the buttons on his trousers open.

"And I just suppose I might be able to think up a way for you to thank me right back," she whispered, a hint of mischief in her voice.

She took her time unfastening the buttons, her fingers moving in slow, teasing motions along the material and through to the hardening manhood below.

After what seemed like a long time, she finally reached her smooth, small hand into the opening of his trousers, and taking a firm grip, drew the hardening shaft from its confines. She looked at it resting in her hand for a long time, feeling its pulsing heat. Then, after one wide-eyed look back up to Ki, Amelia bent her head and gently kissed the thick shaft.

The moist heat from her lips and that single kiss seemed to penetrate Ki to the core, and he leaned back against the wall. Slowly, slowly then, she lifted the shaft with two hands and kissed it again, this time at the very tip. She let her lips linger there before reluctantly pulling them away.

Soon she was planting long, moist kisses up and down the entire length of Ki's shaft. Each one seemed to linger just a little longer than the last, until finally she paused for a long time at the very tip before opening her lips wide. Moving her head slightly, she took just the end of his manhood into her mouth, letting it rest in the wet warmth there.

Then, very slowly and teasingly, she slid the shaft another inch or two inside her, before running her tongue around and around the tip in slow, lazy circles.

Ki felt himself stiffen against the door as she continued to run her tongue over the end of his manhood.

She kept at it for what seemed like a very long time, then inched her way forward, bringing the shaft deeper and deeper into her mouth until its entire length was consumed.

Once again she stopped, letting the full length of the shaft rest in her mouth, before pulling away. Inch by inch the glistening shaft emerged from between her lips until all but the very tip was revealed. Slowly, she began to repeat the process, taking the entire length into her mouth.

Soon her head was moving steadily up and down the shaft, her eager tongue working its pleasurable way along the entire length.

As she began to move faster and faster, she reached into Ki's trousers with one hand and began to gently massage his sac. Using just the tips of her fingers, she ran them in smooth circles, around and around, coaxing the pleasure from Ki.

When he could contain his pleasure no more, he let out a low cry and expended himself in her.

They made love twice more that day, once against the wall where Ki had stood, and again in her narrow bed. Each time, she had cried out loudly, so loudly that the sound of it nearly drowned out the dull roar of the engine.

Later, as they lay in Amelia's narrow bed, she was running the tip of one finger across Ki's smooth chest and purring contentedly like a kitten. "Do you really think I have a nice voice?" she asked.

"Yes, you have a very nice voice," Ki answered. "But you must sing what they want to hear."

"I thought they wanted opera," she replied. "That is what I was told they wanted. I was told, very distinctly, to sing arias."

"Sometimes people do not tell you what they want," Ki answered. "Sometimes you must just know."

"I suppose," she said somewhat dreamily. "I suppose it's just hard to know sometimes."

"Yes, it is," Ki said. "But even a good singer who does not sing what an audience wants is worse off than a poor singer who sings what they do want."

"And what do you suppose I should sing?"

Ki thought about it for a long time, trying to remember the people he had seen boarding the boat. "You should sing whatever they are listening to in the saloons and low places," Ki said. "You should sing whatever is of the time."

"But these people, they're—"

"They are wealthy," Ki interrupted. "They feel all their tastes should be as expensive as the clothes they wear and the food they eat."

"Yes?"

"They buy their clothes and their food," Ki continued. "But they cannot buy patience to learn to appreciate your singing. So you must make them feel they are not only listening to something expensive, but something they can understand as well."

"Just maybe you're right, Ki," she answered, already deep in thought about what he said.

★

Chapter 6

They docked in Cairo a little before nine in the
evening. Word had already reached town, brought
by telegraph and no doubt sent by the two men
left behind, of what had happened. There was no
brass band to meet them as they steamed into
the dock, only a grim collection of people, the
kind who regularly are drawn from their homes
to witness a potential tragedy. There was no body,
nothing that signaled the death, so the onlookers
disbanded shortly after the ship docked.

Jessie found Stratton on the deck, giving last-
minute orders to some of the crew. She had gone
without supper, trading it off for the promise of
his late dinner. Now, as she made her appearance
on the deck, Stratton looked at her, his eyes wan-
dering appreciatively over her form.

"Ah, supper is it?" he asked.

"Supper would be delightful," Jessie said. "I
hope you don't mind, but Ki will be joining us."

"Not at all, as long as he joins us at a place of my choosing," the captain said.

Jessie was a little surprised. She had assumed they would join the others at one of the city's popular places. "Oh, and not with the others?"

"Miss Starbuck, I have already seen quite enough of the others," Stratton said.

Ki had entered so quietly that Jessie did not hear him approach, though when Stratton's eyes gazed over her left shoulder, she turned, already half expecting to see Ki.

"That sit well with you, Ki?" Stratton asked. "That you let me choose the restaurant?"

"I have no objection," Ki answered.

Jessie shrugged and followed Ki and Stratton down the gangplank.

There were a few buggies standing nearby, offered by the shipping company for the convenience of passengers. Jessie headed for the nearest buggy, but Stratton continued walking, his long, confident strides leading him toward a row of warehouses. "This is one of my favorites on the river," Stratton said, as Jessie and Ki hurried to catch up with him.

There were a few gaslights nearby, but not many, and when Stratton walked between two great warehouses, it took a moment for Jessie's eyes to adjust to the darkness.

Presently, they emerged from between the warehouses into a narrow, unpaved street. Heavy wagons and generations of horses had pounded down the earth so it was like stone. A few crude shops, offering ship supplies, provisions, and such, lined the street. Large drays rested on either side of the street, as did the remains of barrels and packing crates.

Ki walked cautiously, every muscle in his body attuned to the place, ready for violence.

The captain turned again, leading Jessie and Ki down a dark alley lit only by a single lamp at the opposite end. "I expect this isn't quite what you're accustomed to," Stratton said, obviously taking some measure of enjoyment in Jessie's discomfort at the surroundings.

Indeed, Jessie had been in lower places in her time, though she was worried about not knowing where she was heading. She couldn't help wondering what it was about the captain that made him choose this particular place or route. Was it some trick of his nature that insisted he be the one leading, in command? Certainly, if they had joined the others, he would not have been in command. On his ship he was in command, even of those who had retained his services, but on land, he was just another employee, no different than the lowest clerk or bookkeeper.

There were several large impressions at the center of the alley, which forced them to walk close to the brick and board sides of the building. When they were halfway to the light at the end, Stratton took a large step forward, then turned easily and said, "Look out for old Jenks, there."

Jessie saw the form of the man, obviously drunk and asleep, sprawled against the wall, just in time, and stepped over his outstretched legs. Ki did likewise.

"I take it that he is one of our fellow patrons?" Jessie asked.

"Hell, no," Stratton said.

Jessie let out a long sigh of relief.

"He's the owner," Stratton continued. "Least he was a few years back. Lost the place in a poker game. Funny how a man's life can turn when he's holding a flush and the fella across the table is holding a full house."

Jessie gave a backward glance down the alley, then turned and watched as Stratton pulled open the heavy door. Instantly, a rush of music, smoke, and the twin aromas of food and alcohol flowed through the opening.

Stratton smiled and stepped into the room.

It was not nearly as bad as Jessie had supposed. The room was low-beamed and noisy, but it seemed well-kept enough. Whatever rats there might have been had the good sense to keep out of sight. Eight or nine low tables and crude chairs were filled with rough-looking men, dock workers and laborers, Jessie guessed.

The captain received a warm welcome from all who saw him and then took a seat at an empty table. Jessie and Ki pulled up two chairs.

In one of the far corners, a skinny, consumptive-looking gent came out and began playing a tinny piano. The sound of the ill-tuned instrument filled the room, nearly drowning out the chorus of cursing, laughing voices.

A fat man with a filthy apron covering his bare chest appeared suddenly and welcomed Stratton. It was so loud that Jessie could not hear the exchange, but after much smiling and nodding between them, Stratton turned his attention from the fat man to Jessie and yelled, "Do you like rabbit, Miss Starbuck?"

"As well as anyone, I suppose," Jessie answered, wondering what kind of rabbit a place like this might serve.

"And what about you, Ki?" Stratton yelled. "Do you like rabbit?"

Ki, seeing the futility of an extended type of exchange, merely nodded his approval.

"Excellent!" Stratton cried, and held up three fingers to indicate their orders.

Almost immediately, three huge bowls of thick stew appeared on the table. Accompanying the stew was a loaf of coarse bread and a bottle of thick red wine.

Stratton wasted no time in plunging his spoon into the stew and retrieving a large portion for his mouth. Jessie watched as he took the first bites, then seeing that he had come to no harm, tried a small spoonful herself.

What she tasted amazed her. It was without a doubt the best rabbit stew—any stew—that she had ever tasted. Ki followed suit, and he, too, found the stew delicious.

In almost no time at all they had emptied their bowls and were drinking the second bottle of wine.

Just then, the piano playing stopped and the room grew silent. Jessie looked around and saw that all eyes were trained on the silent piano. "What's going to happen?" she asked, taking a small sip of wine.

"Entertainment," Stratton answered.

Jessie was about to ask what manner of entertainment, when a door to the kitchen was pulled open and a young woman walked through. She was wearing a faded and stained blue satin dress and an ornate hat with a huge feather. She would have looked absurd, had it not been for the great degree of assurance and pride with which she carried herself. Her pale green eyes scanned the room, offering a unspoken challenge to every member of her audience. It was a challenge that these men, of the roughest variety that the river had to offer, did not rise to accept in thought, deed, or voice.

When the woman had positioned herself comfortably by the piano, the musician gave a few notes of introduction and she began to sing. From the woman issued forth a voice of such remarkable clarity and style that it held Jessie in its grasp. She sang songs—the type you'd hear in any saloon—but with such feeling and warmth that you would believe that the ballads of love, loss, and despair were not only felt by the woman, but written by her as well. Nay, Jessie felt that the woman had actually lived those songs, such was the power, beauty, and sincerity of her voice.

The woman held the audience in her spell for the better part of an hour, then withdrew. When she had gone, the piano player circulated through the audience with an ancient derby hat, which the men gladly filled with paper money and coins.

"It is late," Stratton said suddenly, studying a gold watch he had pulled from his pocket. "We should return to the ship."

Jessie and Ki rose in answer to the suggestion.

Leaving the restaurant, the captain and Jessie proceeded ahead, leaving Ki to follow from twenty yards or so behind. A light rain had begun to fall and the narrow alleyways had turned to mud, the uneven surface filling with water. As they turned the corner, two men stepped in front of them, blocking their progress, then a single man came from behind, blocking their escape.

"Evening to you," one of the men in front of Jessie and Stratton said, casually pulling a revolver from his pocket.

Jessie saw they were dressed in the rough clothes of rivermen, but something about their manner didn't entirely convince her that this was the case.

"Now, hand over the money in this direction, and we'll be on our merry ways," the man said.

"Better do what he tells you," Jessie said, though she doubted that money was what they were after.

"Damnable rogues," Stratton spat as he reached into his pocket.

"Mind yourself, what you pull out of that pocket," the thief said. "I wouldn't want to see this lady come to any harm on your account."

As the captain pulled out several gold coins and bank notes and prepared to hand them over, Jessie heard a faint whisper of steel flying through the air. The man behind her let out a scream. Ki's *shuriken* had found its mark. The throwing star embedded itself firmly in the would-be thief's neck, just below the base of the skull. The sharp point of the steel star sent him to the ground in writhing pain, the gun falling from his hand as he fell.

A second later, another whisper of steel cleaved the rain-heavy air, this one passing within an inch of Jessie's ear to bury itself in the silent thief's throat.

It was then that Stratton struck, his left hand snaking out to smash the shocked gunman square in the face. The blow sent him staggering back a step as his finger squeezed down on the trigger. The gunman's bullet grazed the captain across the upper arm.

Meanwhile, Jessie moved forward, aiming a powerful kick at the thief with the *shuriken* in his throat. The toe of her boot caught him high up between the legs, sending him to the ground, unable to scream in pain through severed vocal chords.

The captain struck the gunman again, this time hitting him square in the face as his other hand pulled the gun from his grip. The man fell back, his shoulder striking the wall of the building as the captain threw the gun away.

Jessie was about to deal a final blow to the writhing thief at her feet, when a carriage pulled up at the end of the alleyway.

Suddenly, a shot rang out and Jessie drew her gun, returning fire. At more than twenty-five yards away, the small .38 was practically useless. Two more shots, which she now recognized as a rifle, split the air. The man at Jessie's feet twitched and convulsed as the two big slugs ripped through his back.

The captain was supporting the gunman with one hand and preparing to strike him him with the other. Suddenly, there was another shot and the gunman went limp, falling as dead weight from Stratton's hand in a heap.

Jessie let fly with three more shots, frightening the horses that pulled the carriage as the lead split the wood on the carriage. "Run!" she screamed as she backed off around the corner, the captain following suit.

A moment later, they heard the carriage pull away, the sound of galloping horses echoing in the distance.

As Jessie and Stratton pressed themselves against the wall, Ki joined them, another *shuriken* ready in his hand. "That was no simple robbery," he said.

Jessie peeked out from behind the corner and saw only the dead men on the ground. "I think you're right, Ki, they knew where we were. They were waiting for us."

"Nonsense," Stratton protested. "The riverfront is full of rats like those, waiting for someone to wander into their path."

"Are these river rats also waiting with a carriage?" Jessie asked.

"Probably just a gent passing through on his way home from a bawdy house, if you'll excuse my expression."

"Then why didn't he stop?" Jessie asked.

"More than likely, you shooting at him had something to do with it," Stratton argued. "And for another thing, he probably didn't want anyone to know he was down here."

"Is that what you intend to believe?" Jessie asked.

"It is," Stratton answered. Then he lifted his arm to massage it, but as he pulled his fingers away, he discovered blood. He had been shot.

★

Chapter 7

Stratton sat on the edge of his bunk as Jessie
slowly eased his jacket off. The garment itself was
ruined. A large gaping hole rimmed with blood
was quite evident just above the elbow. Beneath
the jacket was a clean blue shirt, another hole,
and more blood.

Jessie tore the shirt neatly from the hole,
exposing the wound. It was not as bad as she had
supposed, and not nearly as bad as it might have
been. The wound had already stopped bleeding,
leaving a furrow that was small but ugly.

"Now you shall have something to show all your
lady friends," Jessie teased, cleaning the wound
with a fresh length of linen and grain alcohol.

The captain winced as the alcohol spread into
the raw flesh of the wound. "And what might
lead you to believe that there are lady friends
or, for that matter, lady friends who would be
interested?"

"Are you attempting to tell me there is a drought of lady friends?" Jessie asked, then pressed a length of alcohol-soaked linen square against the wound in punishment for coyness.

"I deny nothing." The captain gasped in pain. "Neither do I admit anything. But I will, upon threat of further pain, ask why you would believe any lady would be interested in a wound!"

"A wound, no," Jessie said, as she began to bandage his arm. "I hardly know of a lady who can resist a scar."

"Ah," Stratton said as the bandage's wrapping grew tighter around his arm.

"There is a problem," Jessie said. "You must have a story to accompany what will make it a fine, heroic scar."

"The truth," Stratton said. "I will tell them the truth."

"Not very exciting and certainly not romantic."

"The war, then?" Stratton suggested.

Jessie shook her head, then rose from her knees. "Much too common."

"River pirates and a mighty battle," Stratton suggested.

"These would be women, not ten-year-old boys."

"A duel! I would have fought a duel with a Frenchman!"

"Better," Jessie said, musing, a half-smile breaking out across her face.

"A duel over a beautiful woman," Stratton continued.

"Much better." Jessie nodded with approval.

"A beautiful, rich woman," Stratton tried.

"Yes, yes," Jessie said.

"Not only beautiful and rich, but royalty as well!"

"Yes, but don't tell it to any lady friend over the age of twenty," she said. "Women may be romantic, but they certainly are not fools. Never insult or betray a woman's sense of romance with your own sense of foolishness. Even women who love romance aren't stupid."

"Is that advice from one who knows?" Stratton asked.

"It's advice that has served men well through the years," Jessie said.

"To think that my romantic life could be improved through a robbery," Stratton mused. "It is a strange world."

Jessie was quiet for a moment. "I don't think it was a robbery," she said. "At least that wasn't the aim of those men."

The captain's face displayed surprise. "They held us under threat of a gun and demanded our money," he said. "If it wasn't intended as a robbery, then what would you call that?"

"I would call it a murder disguised as a robbery," she answered immediately.

"You have a vivid imagination, Miss Starbuck."

"If I do, then why did they not ask for my money?" she answered. "And isn't it curious to think about that waiting carriage? If the man with the rifle intended to rescue us, why did he ride off like that? I believe they intended to kill you and leave me as a witness."

"A witness to what? My murder?" Stratton asked skeptically.

"Exactly," Jessie responded. "It wouldn't be the first time a ship's captain would have met with foul play in an alley. I would have verified the account unwittingly. But then when we got the better of them—"

"With no small thanks to Ki, I might add," Stratton broke in.

"It was necessary to kill their own men," Jessie neatly concluded. "What other explanation is there?"

"A very complicated theory," Stratton said.

"But it all fits," Jessie countered.

"Except for one small detail."

"Which is?"

"Why would anyone want me dead?"

Jessie thought about it for a long time, then said, "That's what I intend to find out, Captain Stratton."

"You do that," Stratton answered. "And when you find the answer, be sure to tell me. I'd be greatly interested in why someone would take the trouble to try to kill me."

By now the bandage was firmly in place and the blood cleaned away from the arm. Jessie had to admit to herself that Stratton was a fine figure of a man, and the bandage, which neatly confined the tight rope of muscles on his arm, did nothing to diminish his appeal.

"Well, Captain, there's nothing more I can do for you here," she said, rising to leave.

"Oh, I wouldn't say that," Stratton answered.

Those were just the words that Jessie had hoped to hear. "Do you need some other attention?" she asked in mock coyness.

"I would wager that given enough time I might possibly be able to think of something," Stratton answered, rising from the bed.

"Anything specific?" Jessie prompted, taking a step toward him.

Stratton also took a step forward so that they were nearly touching. The captain stood so close that Jessie could feel the heat rising off his naked, well-muscled torso. Whether it was the wound or the heat of the closed cabin, Jessie didn't know, but the captain had a fine sheen of sweat glistening over his chest and stomach.

"Is this the sort of attention you require?" she asked in a dramatically coy way, as she eased herself into his arms.

"It would amount to a start, I imagine," Stratton answered as he closed his good arm around her and bent his head to kiss her already slightly parted lips.

They stood like that for a long time, lips together in a passionate embrace. At the first touch of his lips, Jessie could feel his manhood rising under the cloth of his trousers. It poked defiantly upward, touching her just above the belt buckle.

As they continued to kiss, Jessie reached one hand downward and began to unfasten his belt. Her long, smooth fingers worked nimbly over the buttons and brass belt buckle, then slipped comfortably inside his trousers, where she took his hardening shaft in her hand.

Stratton let out a small moan with the first touch of her fingers, slowly breaking off the kiss.

"Is everything all right, Captain?" she asked, as she continued to massage the shaft. "You are not in any pain, are you?"

"No, no pain," he moaned throatily. "It's just, at this moment, I feel the need to sit."

Without releasing her hold on his manhood, Jessie eased him back a step so he was nearly touching the bed. "I would suggest that you sit," she said, gently pushing him back on the bed.

Kneeling down before him, Jessie lifted one of his feet and removed the boot, then she moved on to the next foot. When he was barefoot, she rose slightly and began pulling off his trousers. He obliged by lifting his legs up off the bed as they eased down over his muscular legs.

In moments, he was naked before her. She felt a surge of excitement, suddenly aware of her clothed state. "I can see one part of you that's apparently healthy," she said, eyes fixed on his rigid manhood.

Stratton rose up on one arm and surveyed the member with a casual, familiar eye. "What would you suggest?" he asked. "I would think a closer examination would be in order."

In answer, Jessie knelt between his parted legs, took the stiff organ and gently began to massage it with two hands. Then, when she had comfortably settled herself, she leaned forward and kissed the thick shaft at its base, letting her lips linger there for a long time.

Stratton let out a long moan and reclined far back in the bunk, putting himself at the mercy of her amorous favors.

Jessie poked the tip of her tongue out from between her full lips and slowly began to trace a thin line up the underside of his rigid shaft. She worked her way up, the pink tip of her tongue pausing here and there to play against the sensitive flesh.

When she reached the top of his shaft, she opened her lips slightly and began kissing it, slowly, shyly at first. Then when she had thoroughly kissed the entire crown of the shaft, she opened her mouth and drew him into her.

The captain drew himself up off the bed to meet the warm, moist mouth, but Jessie lifted her head in time to his thrusts so that she was able to take him into her with a slow, teasing pace of her own choosing.

When she had completely taken the captain's manhood into her moist, willing mouth, she paused for a long time, feeling the warm pulse of his desire deep inside her. Then she slowly began to lift her head, letting the hard shaft slide over her silken tongue and from between her soft, full lips.

Stratton groaned again, as nearly the last bit of the now glistening shaft emerged from between Jessie's lips. She held the end firmly between her lips and set her tongue skimming across it this way and that in a passionate dance before taking him completely back inside her mouth.

Soon she was moving her mouth up and down his thick shaft in long, regular strokes. The firm shaft, now glistening, moved smoothly between her full lips. When Jessie sensed that he was close, she raised her hand and began teasing the soft sac between his legs with the tips of her fingers. Then, working her hand up slowly, she began pumping in perfect time to the movement of her mouth.

No more than a minute passed, when Stratton's back arched sharply off the bed and he let out a long moan as he spent himself within her mouth.

For a long time, Jessie let the entire shaft rest inside her mouth, her tongue slowly working its way up and down. Soon, she felt the shaft begin to shrink and she lifted her head from it as she rose to her feet. A second later, she was curled in the crook of Stratton's arm, her hand toying with a strand of smooth hair along his chest.

"I hope that might have taken some of the sting out of getting shot," she said.

"It did, indeed," Stratton answered, his eyes still closed. "I would say that was just what the doctor ordered."

Instantly it hit Jessie. "Shouldn't we have the doctor look at it?" she asked. "Just to be safe."

"Wittick? I wouldn't let him examine a sick cat," Stratton said.

"I take it you don't trust the good doctor."

"Ha! I'd bet whatever you choose, he's never been called that before! Good doctor is the last thing that rascal is," Stratton pronounced, now opening his eyes to look at Jessie. "Went to some fancy Eastern school and the only thing he's good for is putting laudanum into rich widows."

"Doesn't sound like much of a medical practice," Jessie commented.

"Oh, it pays well enough, don't doubt that," Stratton said. "Don't doubt it for a second. Especially if you have the right rich widows. But the man couldn't set a bone if his life depended on it. Believe me, you did what he couldn't do in a year, the way you fixed up my arm."

"Well, thank you, Captain," Jessie said.

"And your bedside manner is something that just makes a man want to go out and get shot every day, if he could," Stratton said. "Of course, then he might leak like a damned net, but it'd be worth it."

Chapter 8

Jessie came down from her cabin in the morning to find Givens, the gambler, playing cards with Delamore at a corner table in the salon. Both men were stripped down to their shirtsleeves, a stubble of beard gracing their faces. It looked likely that they'd been playing cards through-out the night and were now beginning on their second day.

The ship was already well under way, the scen-ery gliding by at a slow, steady pace outside the large windows.

As she made her way into the dining room, she noted that the captain was seated with the inves-tors at the head table. It was Seacrest who spotted her first, pausing only briefly from his plate of food to offer her an acknowledgment. Presently, as she approached the table, Stratton, Stempley, and Moran also acknowledged her. Strope was oblivious. Already having consumed his day's ration of liquor, he was lost in his own drunken thoughts.

"The good captain was just telling us of your little adventure last night," Stempley said, smiling. "Ah, to be young again and meet the world head-on."

"It sounds like the 'world' nearly got the better of them," Moran observed.

"Nearly," Jessie answered, "but not quite."

"It might interest you to know that the local officials have already paid a visit, before we got under way," Stempley said. "We managed to persuade them that it would not be in their best interest to wake you."

"Who reported the murders?" Jessie asked as a cup of coffee appeared in front of her, placed there by one of the linen-outfitted stewards.

"I did," Stratton answered. "They had more questions about Ki's weapons than about the men. It seems they were well-known to the authorities."

"And the man in the carriage?" Jessie asked.

"Still a mystery," Stratton answered.

Jessie took a sip of her coffee, the eggshell-thin cup unsteady in her hand. "How long have they been at it out there?" she asked, indicating Delamore and Givens.

"Since last night," Stempley said. "If our good Mr. Givens isn't careful, he could end up owning a share in the ship."

"That bad, is it?" Seacrest muttered with a mouthful of food.

"The last time I inquired, he owed Givens approximately five thousand dollars," Stempley said. "That was last night, past midnight."

"I asked him myself, this morning," Seacrest said. "Delamore told me to mind my own damned business. I imagine he owes him quite a bit more by now."

"I'd wager on that," Stempley said.

"And Mr. Delamore would probably accept the bet," Stratton countered, his small joke bringing chuckles of dark delight to the other men.

Then, as if on cue, Delamore and Givens entered the dining room. Jessie noted that, except for the beard, Givens looked fresh, as if he'd just dressed. He walked with a light spring to his step and there was an odd spark of life in his eye. Delamore, however, walked in a slouched shuffle, his eyes dulled from futile concentration.

"'Morning, gentlemen, Miss Starbuck," Givens said, taking a seat. "I trust you all had the benefit of a good night's sleep."

"That's more than you can say," Jessie answered.

"Unfortunately, correct, Miss Starbuck," Givens answered. "But I plan to avail myself of it shortly."

"No, you don't," Delamore said suddenly. "We're going to keep playing."

Givens offered Delamore and the others at the table the small smile of a reasonable man dealing with an unreasonable one. "There'll be plenty of time for amusement," he said. "We still have days for it."

"Oh, that's the way it is, then," Delamore said. "You're the type to skin a man, then back out, just when the luck is moving to the other side of the table? You're the type to not give a man a chance? Is that the way it is?"

"Sir, I've offered you every chance," Givens said. "And I will continue to do so, but not until I have rested."

"Like hell! We'll keep playing now!" Delamore snarled, causing several of the nearby diners to turn their heads at the outburst. "We'll keep playing now or you won't see a penny of what you won. Is that clear to you, Mr. Givens?"

The men around the table held their breath. It looked as if it might come to some piece of ugliness between Delamore and Givens. Finally, Givens said, "Perfectly clear, Mr. Delamore. As soon as I finish my coffee, we shall resume."

The crisis temporarily quelled, Stratton rose from his seat and announced, "If you gentlemen will excuse me, I have a ship to see to."

Delamore stormed out of the dining room as the steward poured Givens his coffee. The gambler took a small sip from the cup, aware that every eye in the room was fastened on him, then rose. "I should oblige our impatient Mr. Delamore," Givens said to no one in particular. Rising with a sort of weary dignity, he exited the room, holding his coffee cup.

"It's a sickness, nothing more than that," Strope said drunkenly. "Horrible, ugly thing to witness."

"You would know," Seacrest said.

"And just what is that intended to mean?" Strope shot back bitterly.

"Just that you never stray far from the bottle, as our dear Mr. Delamore from his cards," Seacrest offered by way of explanation.

"What about that fancy, toad-eating cook you drag around like a wife?" Strope sputtered.

"Gentlemen, gentlemen," Moran said in an attempt to calm both men.

"And just who do you think you are?" Seacrest spat. "You with your whores are not one to—"

Before Moran could respond, they were aware of a terrible fight coming from the salon. Jessie leapt from her seat and was through the door in time to see Givens holding a gun on Delamore. The table on which they had played their game was overturned.

"You're wrong, friend," Givens said, the tiny pearl-handled revolver clutched in his hand.

"Wrong, am I, you cheating bastard?" Delamore yelled. "Those cards are marked, plain as day. A blind man could see it."

"That's not my deck, friend," Givens answered.

"You want me to believe that? You thieving cheat, don't insult me twice!"

Jessie noticed that even though Givens was the one holding the gun, he looked more frightened. She had seen cheats caught before, and they didn't act like Givens.

"Now, just calm down," Givens said, soothingly. "If there's a question of the winnings, I shall be glad to return the money."

"Ha! So you admit cheating me!"

"Sir, I admit nothing."

"Why, you lying bastard," Delamore shouted,

then went for the pocket of his coat, which was slung over the back of the chair.

Givens took a quick step back, but he didn't fire. Perhaps he was hoping against hope that Delamore wasn't going for his gun.

When the gun, a two-shot pocket model, did appear, Givens shouted, "Don't, you fool!"

Delamore paid no mind to the warning, perhaps thinking that Givens was too cowardly to shoot. He was wrong. As Delamore raised the small gun, Givens fired a shot that struck the investor high in the chest. He staggered back a step as the bullet ripped into him, but he did not fall.

A mild look of surprise passed over Delamore's face and he continued to raise the gun, taking unsteady aim with the pistol.

The shot had struck Delamore directly in the heart. He stood wavering for a second, looking from Givens to his own gun, then fell. He was dead by the time he hit the floor.

"You saw what happened!" Givens said, turning to Jessie and the crowd gathered at her back. "You all saw it. He was insane over losing."

Jessie nodded slowly as a low murmur went through the crowd behind her.

"Put it down, now!" Stratton's voice boomed from the other end of the salon.

Moving her gaze from Givens, Jessie saw the captain in the opposite doorway, a shotgun up at his shoulder, pointed directly at Givens.

The gambler smiled slightly, then stooped to carefully lay his gun down on the floor.

"Now, move away from it," Stratton ordered.

Givens took several steps away from the gun and turned his back to Stratton.

The captain, satisfied, lowered the shotgun and strode into the room. When he reached Delamore, he bent down, still holding the scattergun, and felt for a pulse. There wasn't one.

"Somebody run and fetch Wittick!" Stratton ordered to no one in particular, though with an attitude of command that assumed it would be done. Then, to Jessie, "Did you see what happened, Miss Starbuck?"

The formality of his address would have struck Jessie as strange under any other circumstance. "Yes. Mr. Delamore threatened Mr. Givens with a gun," she said.

"Looks just the other way around, if you ask me," Stratton answered, rising.

Wittick entered then, surveyed the scene briefly, and ran to the body. Bending, he searched for a pulse, found none, then made his official pronouncement, "He's dead."

"Then there's nothing you can do for him," Stratton said. "Move on away from him."

Wittick did as he was told, joining the crowd that stood behind Jessie.

"Mr. Givens already had his gun out when Delamore went for the pistol in his coat pocket," Jessie elaborated.

"It was a fool's move," Givens said. "The odds were badly against him."

"Shut up," Stratton ordered. "When I want to hear from you, I'll ask you directly."

"Delamore accused him of cheating," someone in the crowd behind Jessie said.

"Is that true, Miss Starbuck?" Stratton asked, assuming Jessie to be the most reliable witness.

Jessie nodded in answer, then said, "Delamore thought the cards were marked."

Stratton knelt down and gathered up the cards scattered across the floor around the overturned table, body, and broken coffee cup. Arranging the cards in his hand, he flipped through them quickly, running a finger down the outside of one side and then the other. Then he repeated the process a second time, to be certain.

"Well, was they marked?" someone called from the crowd.

"They were," Stratton said, then threw the marked cards to the floor in disgust.

"Impossible! You're lying!" Givens shouted, turning suddenly, which caused Stratton to wheel back around to level the gun at him.

"Am I?" Stratton asked. "Am I lying? See for yourself."

Givens scurried over to the scattered cards and gathered them up. Then he performed the same test on them that Stratton had, flipping them quickly as he studied the backs to see if the pattern changed. It did. A look of horror and disgust spread across his face. "I—I don't understand," he said at last. "There's no explanation. None at all."

"Yes, there is," Stratton said.

"These aren't the same cards we were playing with," Givens offered. "They couldn't be."

Stratton didn't answer. He bent down, picked up Delamore's gun, and checked the load, his face impassive.

"I don't understand it, Captain," Givens pleaded, still holding the cards. "It doesn't make any sense."

"Doesn't it?" Stratton asked, raising Delamore's gun so that it pointed at Givens.

"Captain, what . . . what do you intend to do?" Givens asked, as Stratton took careful aim at the gambler, his finger firm around the trigger.

"What do you suppose the penalty for killing an unarmed man would be?" Stratton asked.

"Don't do it, please, for the love of mercy, no!" Givens begged.

Stratton pulled back on the trigger, the hammer moving slowly away from the pistol's frame.

"No! Please!" Givens yelled, as the hammer came back, clicking down on a spent shell.

★

Chapter 9

An hour after the shooting, Jessie found Stratton on the bridge, his hands fastened to the wheel and his eyes gazing out over the river. "Miss Starbuck," he said, without turning from his post. "There was a time, not long ago, when it was much easier to be on the river."

"Where's Givens?" Jessie asked.

"Don't fear, Jessie," Stratton answered. "We haven't thrown old Jerome over the side. I've just ordered him confined to his cabin, a measure that should protect him from the others."

"I don't think he did it," Jessie said.

"Would that be cheat with marked cards or slip a used cartridge into Delamore's pistol?"

"Either," Jessie responded. "I don't think he'd do either one. I saw the way he tried to avoid shooting Delamore."

"And the manner in which he cowered in front of Delamore's gun?" Stratton added. "If he'd slipped that shell into the chamber, he'd have no cause for fear, would he?"

"Then you believe his story?" Jessie asked. She had no affection for the gambler, but it pained her to think that an innocent man would be accused of murder. That was intolerable, no matter what his profession might be.

"Jerome has been on the river for years," Stratton said. "He's been skinning men like Delamore and making a pretty good living at it for as long as I can remember. In all those years I've never known him to be involved in anything like this. He's never been one for marked cards or gunplay. To be perfectly blunt, he doesn't have any need to mark cards to extract his money from men like Delamore."

"Then what do you suppose happened?" Jessie asked.

"I wouldn't care to speculate," Stratton answered. "I'm a ship's captain, not a sheriff, marshall, or Pinkerton agent. I know that one man is dead. The ship now belongs to two less men and we have two days to reach Memphis."

Jessie was about to say something, when suddenly Seacrest burst onto the bridge. "Captain, I must protest this outrage," he blustered. "I've just been informed of the location of the departed Mr. Delamore and I, as well as my chef, find it totally unacceptable."

"He's staying put, Mr. Delamore," Stratton answered without turning from the wheel.

"Totally unacceptable," Seacrest said. "As an investor in this ship, and your superior, I order you to relocate him immediately."

"Mr. Seacrest, what would you like me to do?" Stratton answered. "Have him tricked up in a formal dining suit and seated at your table? Would that satisfy your sense of propriety?"

"Where is he?" Jessie asked.

"In the ice compartment!" Seacrest exclaimed. "They put him in with the provisions. I must insist that something be done."

"What would you like done?" Stratton asked. "Exactly what would you like done about it? As you may have noticed, it's a lovely day. I can set him up on deck, but no doubt he'll be better than a little ripe by the time we reach Memphis."

"Deposit him with the local authorities, then," Seacrest suggested.

"We can fight that current back upriver," Stratton said. "It will cost you some. But if I try to dock anywhere along here, we'll run aground so badly it will cost two, maybe three days."

"Then back upriver we must head, immediately," Seacrest insisted.

"I'm afraid you've been outvoted," Stratton answered politely. "The others want to keep heading toward Memphis."

"Ah, what do they care if Delamore drips his insides over my fois gras?" he fumed. "I'll talk to them, you can be certain of that!" Seacrest stormed from the bridge, off to have a few words with his fellow investors.

"Sometimes, Jessie, it just makes me want to go back to hauling nothing but cargo," Stratton sighed. "Sometimes I'd rather pilot a barge of swine than a sidewheeler full of rich folks."

In the salon, the blood still visible on the floor, she met up with Stempley.

"Terrible shame," he said. "About Delamore, that is."

"Yes," Jessie answered. "More than a shame. I think it was murder."

"Of course," Stempley answered, a grim smile playing across his face. "You saw it. Of course it was murder."

"No, I think someone planted those cards," Jessie said. "I think someone planted those cards at the table and emptied Delamore's gun."

Stempley jolted at what Jessie said, clearly taken aback by her theory. "A river gambler cheating? A gentleman of leisure not loading his gun? Either event is hardly news, dear girl."

"And together, they are what? Coincidence?"

"Exactly. Tragic coincidence," Stempley insisted. Then, to turn the moment lighter, he said, "I must talk to Ki about that active imagination of yours. I wasn't aware of that particular Starbuck trait."

If he didn't already know of the attack in the alley the previous night, Jessie wasn't going to enlighten him. Even if she did mention it, he would chalk that up to an active imagination as well. "Speaking of Ki, have you seen him?" she asked, wanting now to change the subject.

Stempley thought for a moment, then said, "The last time I saw him, he was escorting Amelia, that entertainer, back to her cabin."

Jessie had a pretty good idea what Ki's purpose was in going with the singer back to her cabin. Although she needed to speak to him about Delamore and Givens, she knew better than to interrupt whatever amorous meeting he had arranged. She would have to speak with him later, when he had emerged from the woman's cabin.

"What now, dear girl?" Stempley asked. "Care to entertain an old man with a game of chess?"

"I'm afraid just now that I have this crashing headache," she said, sorry for the lie, but knowing she would not be able to keep her mind on a chessboard. "Perhaps in a few hours."

"Very well, then," Stempley replied, only slightly disappointed.

Jessie excused herself and headed back to the cabins. She felt that perhaps if she spoke with Givens, he could cast some light on the situation.

She was halfway down the main corridor when she saw Moran approaching. "Miss Starbuck, what a delightful meeting," Moran said, blocking her way.

Jessie wasn't quite sure what he was talking about, but the leer on his face gave her a pretty good idea. "Yes, now if you'll excuse me—" she said, attempting to move around the man.

"Dreadful shame about old Delamore, isn't it?" Moran said.

"Yes, it is," Jessie answered.

"Puts one in mind to contemplate the fleeting quality of life and all that, doesn't it?"

"I'm certain it does."

"How we should snatch every pleasure possible, and without hesitation," Moran continued.

Jessie ceased her attempt to escape, seeing it was hopeless. "I'm not certain what you're getting at, Mr. Moran, but I'm sure it would make for fascinating dinner conversation. Now, if you'll excuse me—"

Moran smiled wider. "What I'm getting at, Miss Starbuck, is that it's been a day, perhaps more, since I've had a woman," he said. "I find it a marvelous and glad coincidence that you just happen to be a woman."

Jessie was stunned but not surprised by the directness of his approach. "Mr. Moran—"

"No, no, no, don't refuse me immediately," he said. "Think about it. I insist that you seriously entertain the idea. I have a weak heart. It would not require much exertion."

"I will, then," Jessie said, renewing her attempt at escape.

Moran paused, seemed to let his guard down, but still did not let her pass. "Have you thought of about it?" he asked, smiling lewdly.

"Yes, and the answer is no," Jessie said, pushing her way past the man.

Just as she squeezed by, Moran reached for her. It was, he soon discovered, a mistake. Punching out quickly, Jessie landed a blow directly across his ribs, which doubled him over with a gasp.

As she fled down the hall, Moran cried out, "A woman with spirit! I like that. But remember, I have a weak heart!"

Turning the corner, Jessie found a burly crewman standing guard at Givens's room. "Ma'am," was all he said at her approach.

"I'd like to talk to Mr. Givens, if you don't mind," Jessie said.

"I'm afraid I can't let you in," the crewman answered. "The captain told me he's not to have visitors."

"Well, the captain asked me to bring some of his papers to the bridge," Jessie lied. "He thinks the authorities in Memphis might be interested in them."

"I really shouldn't—" the man said, uncertain now of his position.

"Trust me. I'll assume full responsibility," Jessie said.

"Well, in that case, I think I can let you in," he said, and pulled open the door.

Inside the room, Jessie found Givens stretched out on his bed, reading a book.

"And to what do I owe this pleasure?" the gambler asked, more than a little amused by Jessie's appearance in his cabin.

"I was wondering if you had any idea who would want Delamore dead," she explained, then took a seat at the other side of the small room.

"I couldn't imagine," Givens answered. "If, in fact, that was the object of the entire plot."

"What else could it be?"

"To discredit me," Givens said. "A gambler is perfectly respectable work on these boats. Up until very recently, I provided a welcome source of entertainment. To be a cheat, that is unacceptable entirely. Nobody welcomes a cheat on a boat. It is, very simply, bad for business."

"So you think the marked cards were planted there to discredit you?" Jessie asked, knowing that the theory was based more on Givens's inflated self-esteem than on facts.

"Exactly. What other explanation could there possibly be?" he answered. "This boat could have been a floating gold mine for me. Now, it is nothing but a shabby bunch of timbers floating down a river. Marvelous how our perceptions can change so quickly, isn't it?"

"That might explain the marked cards, but why remove the bullets from Delamore's gun?" Jessie asked. "If he killed you, then your competition would have you out of the way permanently, wouldn't they?"

Givens frowned slightly. "Interesting point, isn't that?" he answered. "A point well worth pondering at length."

"Let me ask you something," Jessie said. "Who would want Delamore dead?"

"Certainly not I," Givens replied quickly. "He was a man who inherited his wealth and, happily, none of the brains of his ancestors. A gambler doesn't kill such a man. Indeed, any man I know who earns his fortune by the graces of lady chance would offer his own right hand to keep such a man alive. To kill him means that the fortune would pass out of his inept control into—"

"Of course," Jessie exclaimed. "His heirs!"

"Sadly, Mr. Delamore has no heirs," Givens replied. "Nor wife, nor relatives. He was indeed a sad individual, alone in the world, with only two or three million dollars to offer him comfort."

★

Chapter 10

"But Ki, I don't understand," Amelia said. "Where did you find all of this music?"

"I happened to discover it in the piano bench," he answered.

Amelia sat on the bed next to Ki and paged through the sheet music, her nose wrinkling in mild dissatisfaction at what she found. "But this is popular music," she said. "I can't sing this. These are really no more than music hall songs."

"Yes," Ki said. "I would suggest that you learn these to sing. They will like them."

"But Ki, poor, sweet Ki, you just don't understand," she said, her fingers lightly caressing his face. "I am an opera singer. I have trained in New York."

"This is what they will like," he answered. "If you are to please them with your singing, you must sing what they like."

"But popular songs?" she replied, saying the word as if it were painful.

"You should try," Ki said. "If they do not like them, then nothing is lost."

"Very well, then," Amelia relented. "After my aria tonight I shall sing a popular song."

Ki allowed himself a rare smile and began to rise off the bed. "You shall see, they will like it," he said.

"I said I'll try it," Amelia replied, then reached out a hand to sit Ki back down. "In any event, it was so sweet of you to bring them."

"I do not want you to fail," he said.

Amelia unfastened the first button of his loose-fitting shirt. "And that's so sweet," she purred. "Just so nice."

Ki didn't answer, but waited as she slipped her hand inside his shirt to let her fingers roam across his hairless chest, feeling the muscles beneath the smooth skin.

A little while later, they were both reclining on the bed. Ki's shirt was nearly entirely removed, and Amelia was planting kiss after kiss across his smooth chest.

Ki reached across and felt her full, firm breast. Instantly, the nipple hardened against the palm of his hand. Amelia purred again. Ki leaned across and began unfastening the tiny pearl-colored buttons that ran up and down the entire length of the dress. When he had unfastened every button down to her waist, he slipped his hand into the dress and felt her breast again through the silken undergarment. It rose hard and defiantly against his palm as he rubbed it gently.

Amelia let out a soft sigh as Ki slipped his hand across her chest and rubbed her other nipple, feeling the warm fullness of her breast against his hand.

"Oh, Ki, you are a devil," she moaned, her hips rising slightly in pleasure. "You are the devil."

Leaning across, he let his lips trail across her smooth, scented skin, just touching the pale flesh where her hairline began above the ear.

She could feel his warm, moist breath and soft, cool lips against her flesh. Little by little, he worked his way across the outside of her ear, lightly kissing her skin. Each touch felt warmer, more exciting than the last, until he began working his way slowly down her neck. He continued his sensual journey until his lips touched the finely trimmed collar of her undergarment, then began tracing a soft trail of kisses around that.

"Oh, Ki, let me," she purred. "Let me do something for you. Please."

Ki shook his head softly in answer, but did not stop. Presently, his lips came upon the gentle upward curve of her breast. Then, lifting his head slightly, he ceased for a moment, only to begin again when he brought his lips to rest on her firm nipple.

With the utmost gentleness he let the solid nipple, encased in satin, slide between his lips. Then he gently began teasing it with careful bites, using only his lips. He played with the thick nipple between his lips for a long time, then rose up slightly and turned his attention to the other.

Now, leaning over her, he let his hand trace a teasing trail down her side, then slowly up across her waist. Finally, his hand slipped into the drawstring opening of her undergarment and searched out her secret, downy moistness.

"Oh, Ki, please," Amelia begged. "Please, take me now. Now!"

For a long moment Ki hesitated, letting just the tips of his fingers play gently in the silken thatch. He could feel her quiver and roll under each touch, and his fingers delved deeper and deeper into her female moistness.

"Ki, please, I fear I can't stand it much longer. Please," she begged, as her hips rolled and undulated upward to meet each passionate and playful touch.

Reluctantly pulling his hand from her undergarment, Ki rose up off the bed and unfastened his trousers. Amelia, through smoldering eyes, took in the aroused manhood as Ki hastily kicked the garment away across the floor. Then, very gently, he bent and pulled the dress from Amelia as she raised her hips to help in the pleasant task.

Without hesitation, she raised her hips once again and slipped off her undergarment. "Take me now, please," she moaned.

Before Ki could bend to open her long legs, she was back up on the bed, kneeling. "Like this, take me like this," she begged, raising her buttocks to him enticingly.

Stepping forward, Ki gently held on to either side of her thin hips, his rigid staff poking between her soft thighs. Using one hand, Amelia reached back and gently guided him into her, as she pushed her entire body back to meet him.

Inch by inch, Ki sank into her warm wetness as she slowly began to rock back and forth. Before long he was moving faster and faster, pulling himself nearly completely out before gently sliding back in.

"Ki, Ki, Ki, that feels so—so very good," she moaned.

In answer, Ki bent forward, then reached around and took one of her full, firm breasts in his hand. His fingers eagerly sought out the thick nipple, pulling and teasing it as it hung down.

Then he felt her begin to shake. She let out a muffled cry as Ki worked himself faster and faster. When he finally spent himself within her, she, too, reached her moment.

A second later, she collapsed on the bed, Ki's manhood falling out of her. He leaned down then, climbing back into the bunk as he curled into her from behind.

"Oh, that was just wonderful, Ki," she whispered. "Wonderful."

"Yes, it was," Ki answered, still slightly short of breath. "It was wonderful."

Jessie, having abandoned Givens to his book and his own dark thoughts, found Strope in the salon. A large bottle of brandy stood before him, and judging from its level, he'd been drinking steadily for some time. In any case, Jessie surmised, he'd been drinking long enough to outlast any drinking companion and chase away any sober one.

"Miss Starbuck! What a wonderful surprise," Strope said, raising his snifter. "Come and join me for a drink."

Jessie crossed the room to Strope with some hesitation as he ordered a steward to bring another snifter for his guest. "Early for a drink, isn't it?" she asked, though she knew that for men like Strope, it was never too early.

"Nonsense," he proclaimed. "I never hold with convention. Never. Especially when it comes to drinking."

A snifter appeared in front of Jessie, and Strope poured a generous helping into it. "Now, what do you think of our little adventure so far?" he asked.

"Well, it's been an awfully long time between untimely deaths," Jessie answered, lifting the snifter.

"Ah, excellent, a woman with a sense of humor," Strope laughed. "I like that! Damn but I like that!"

"Like it or not, don't you find it peculiar?" Jessie asked.

"Extremely. Beautiful women rarely have a decent sense of humor," Strope answered. "Of course, you meet the rare one who can sometimes tell a joke, but for the most part, I would say they are in fact like trained monkeys. Nothing but a damned trained monkey done up in expensive clothes."

"I was referring to the deaths," Jessie corrected, seeing that it was not going to be easy speaking with Strope in his present condition. Unfortunately, his present condition was his usual condition.

"Oh, those," he said, dismissing the deaths of his fellow investors with a wave of a brandy snifter. "Unfortunate accidents. Nothing more. We live in dangerous times. Dangerous and uncertain times, for which the wise man fortifies himself amply."

"Does anyone benefit from those deaths?" Jessie asked.

Strope seemed to think on the question for a long time. "Certainly they don't," he said at last. "Their families perhaps. As I remember, both Quigley and Delamore had large insurance policies against their lives. Then, there is the question of inheritance. I imagine someone would stand to inherit quite a bit of money."

"But no one person?" Jessie asked. "Just their families and such?"

"Just their families," Strope said, taking a large drink from the snifter. "What exactly are you saying, that these weren't accidents?"

"It does seem strange; you yourself would have to admit that fact," she answered.

Strope's face turned from one of the genial drunk to the ugly variety. "Miss Starbuck, you slander their memories with such talk," he said. "I defy you to concoct a manner in which someone would benefit, and benefit well enough to conceive of murder."

"This ship, for instance," Jessie mused. "With two owners deceased, who would get their shares? The remaining investors or the families?"

"Neither, Miss Starbuck," Strope answered, indulging in another large swallow that nearly drained the snifter. "Do not delude yourself into thinking that any of the investors used his own money."

"Do you mean to tell me that you didn't invest in the ship?" Jessie asked.

Strope's eyes glazed over for a moment, his vision becoming unfocused. "No, of course not," he snorted. "What man in his right mind would use his own money in the purchase of a ship? He would have to be insane."

"I'm afraid I don't understand," Jessie said.

"Do you know what a ship is, Miss Starbuck?" he asked, pouring himself a generous portion of brandy into the nearly empty snifter. Apparently Jessie's company had somehow refueled his desire for a drink, though whether it was her mere presence or the conversation, she could not tell.

"A vessel, a boat, a—"

"No, no, no," Strope broke in impatiently. "A ship is a hole in the water into which fools throw their money. That is what a ship is. And believe me, neither I nor my fellow investors are fools."

"Then where exactly did the money come from?" Jessie asked.

"Where'd what money come from?" he answered drunkenly. Strope was already far too drunk to be of use. He'd been drinking steadily for hours, and was reaching that point where he was unable to form clear thoughts. Jessie saw it as a bad piece of luck, but she considered that he might not have been so free in speaking if he had been sober, or relatively sober, when she first approached him.

"The money for the ship—who paid for the ship?" Jessie asked patiently.

"What ship? What idiot would buy a ship?" he replied. "Do you know what a ship is?"

"It's a hole in the water," Jessie answered. "That fools throw their money into."

"Exactly," Strope answered, then promptly lowered his head to the table and fell asleep.

Jessie gently removed the snifter from his hand, recorked the bottle, and attempted to summon a steward to remove the investor to his room.

The two men who finally arrived at the table appeared confident if not well practiced in lifting Strope from his chair and walking him slowly out of the salon and down the narrow corridor.

Jessie rose from her seat, determined to find Stempley or someone else who might be able to tell her what Strope was talking about.

★

Chapter 11

"My dear, you must understand, these matters are very complex," Stempley said. "They are very complex indeed."

"I was curious, however, to know what Strope meant when he said, 'Only fools would invest in a ship,'" Jessie replied.

They were at dinner, seated at the investors' table, which seemed to have grown larger since the beginning of the voyage and the untimely deaths of Quigley and Delamore. Then, too, Strope was also missing, still passed out drunk in his cabin.

"Oh, for the love of mercy, tell her," Seacrest said. "Tell her before she ruins this beautiful meal for me with her badgering."

"Very well, then," Stempley said. "Let us hope you've inherited your father's good head for business. The ship was built as a joint partnership with the men you've met here."

"Including Mr. Quigley and Mr. Delamore," Jessie replied.

"Exactly. We conceived of her and commissioned the plans," Stempley answered. "Once she was built, we undertook her management, including the shipping and passenger business, both of which require thousands of small details. I am not being immodest when I say that it is through her management that she will succeed or fail."

"And who paid for the actual work?" Jessie asked.

"A corporation was formed; the men here, the investors, represent the sole stockholders of that corporation," Stempley continued. "It was that corporation that borrowed the money to build the ship."

"And the money was borrowed from where?"

"Why, a bank, of course," Stempley said, as if speaking to a child. "It is the bank that holds the notes, the stock certificates, as collateral against the loan that built the ship."

"And the loan is paid off through the profits the ship makes," Jessie concluded. "Without any of you putting in one cent."

"Now, now, dear girl, don't judge us so harshly," Stempley said soothingly. "After all, we are providing our expertise as businessmen."

"Damned precious it is, too," Moran said, splitting his undivided attention from the study of Jessie's breasts.

"Damned precious," Seacrest agreed. "The world is run by fools and rascals for the most part. A

101

solid businessman is the last trace of sanity, if you ask me."

"But in the event of an untimely death, who would receive the stock certificates?" Jessie asked. "The family?"

"Ordinarily, yes, the stock would fall into the possession of the deceased's family," Stempley said.

"But not now?" Jessie asked.

"No, not now," Moran answered. "At this point, the bank or the other investors have the right to buy the stock immediately."

This seemed an unusual arrangement to Jessie. Why not just let the stock certificates or share in the boat pass directly to the families of the men who died? "Why was it done differently this time?"

The table fell silent. Apparently none of the men felt comfortable with answering this rather simple question.

"My dear girl, business, as I've explained, is a very complex thing," Stempley finally said. "Sometimes it is as much a matter of human feelings as of finance."

"What, exactly, are you saying?" Jessie answered, determined to get to the heart of the manner. All the flowery talk didn't suit her, not at all.

"Oh, for pity's sake, I'll tell her, before you ruin my parsnips in butter sauce," Seacrest said. "Nobody wanted any family members meddling."

"We are not young men, Jessie," Stempley said. "Together, we can run the ship. However, if the widow or offspring suddenly became a partner—"

"It would ruin everything," Seacrest said. "It's never a question of too many cooks, but the wrong cooks, ruining the stew."

"Just which one of you proposed this arrangement?" Jessie asked.

Moran began laughing and was quickly joined by Stempley and Seacrest. "Funny thing, you should ask that," Seacrest said. "I wouldn't have thought of it, otherwise, but you know, it was Quigley. He insisted on it, actually."

"So his share goes back to the bank?" she asked, just as the laughter was dying down.

"Probably yes," Stempley said. "Speaking only for myself, I have no need for more shares in a ship."

The others chose to play their hands closer to the vest, saying nothing.

Suddenly, Seacrest lowered his fork, his face gone ashen.

"Nelson, are you feeling sick?" Stempley asked.

"Just now, I feel most uncomfortable," he answered with some difficulty. "Most dreadful."

"Perhaps it was something you ate?" Stempley tried.

"Ate? Nonsense, I have the finest chef—" he began, but didn't finish. A second later, after wavering in pain in his seat, he collapsed into his plate of uneaten food.

"Quick! Someone call Wittick!" Jessie yelled.

Almost immediately, the doctor arrived, rushing into the dining room in his shirtsleeves. While the others arranged Seacrest on the floor, the doctor took his pulse, then bent to listen to his breathing.

Jessie watched as the doctor went to work. A moment later, Stratton was at her side.

"Not another one," the captain moaned. "What's wrong with him?"

"If I didn't know better, I'd say he was poisoned," Wittick said as he continued his examination. "What has he eaten?"

"You mean, what hasn't he eaten?" Moran quipped.

"Don't trifle with me," Wittick replied angrily. "What was on his dish?"

"Roast beef in some French sauce, glazed carrots, and uh, parsnips," Jessie answered, taking a quick inventory of the plate.

"Did anyone else eat any of it?" Wittick asked.

The group mumbled no as Seacrest began violently trembling. A second later, one of the stewards burst through the door. "Doctor, it's the Frenchman, he's sick," the man said. "He's sick bad!"

"Get a blanket! Cover him over," Wittick instructed. "I'll see what I can do for the Frenchman."

They did as they were told, Jessie kneeling beside the dying man as he continued to tremble. A few minutes later, he was dead. Jessie shut his eyes.

The rest of the diners had cleared out, leaving only the remaining investors, Jessie, and the body. Ki arrived then, quietly observing the scene for a short time before Jessie took note of him.

"Ki, go tell the doctor that Seacrest is dead," she said.

Without answering, he made for the kitchen. But it wasn't Ki who arrived back in the dining room first, it was the doctor. He strode into the nearly deserted area with a face as grim as death. "Well, he's dead," Wittick said. "That makes two, I suppose."

"What killed them?" Stratton asked.

"Only two people ate that meal," Wittick answered. "Seacrest and the French cook. It must have been something on their plate. But don't ask me what."

Suddenly, a door opened at the opposite end of the room. Ki stood in the opening. "This is what killed them," he said, holding up a bouquet of some sort.

"They were eating leaves?" Moran asked.

"Hemlock," Stratton said in a low voice. "That's hemlock."

"The cook brought it on the boat at Cairo," Ki said. "He thought it was wild parsnips."

"That's impossible," Stratton said. "Even I know that parsnips don't grow around here. What in hell kind of cook was he, anyway?"

"He was French," Ki replied, by way of explanation.

"Now he's dead," Wittick elaborated. "I've had the body placed in the food locker with the other. I suggest you do the same with Mr. Seacrest."

"Well, at least the son of a bitch will feel at home," Moran offered. "Locked in a room with all the food he could want and a Frenchman."

The other members of the group offered harsh stares in reply, but said nothing at all to him. Rather, they summoned stewards to remove the body of their comrade to a temporary resting place in the kitchen.

They stood in the dining room for a long time, after watching the linen-jacketed stewards remove the body. Finally, Stempley turned to Stratton and asked, "What are your immediate plans, Captain?"

"Plans? I plan to pilot this ship to Memphis," Stratton answered. "That is, if you folks could keep from dying long enough for me to run my ship."

"That's a wholly inappropriate comment," Moran said. "Wholly out of line."

"And dying on my ship is totally out of line," Stratton answered. "You folks are dropping like flies and that doesn't suit me one bit."

Having spoken his mind, the captain was gone, striding off in a fit of near fury.

"He does have a point there," Stempley said, after he was certain the captain was beyond earshot. "A quite good one, though rudely expressed."

"Perhaps now you'll consider the possibility that something strange is going on," Jessie said.

"Bad luck is always strange," Stempley replied, and left.

The remainder of the passengers had begun to file back into the dining room and take their seats. Their conversation was in muffled whispers. Apparently a death had not adversely affected their appetites. Immediately after reclaiming their seats, they began to order the stewards to bring them the last portion of their meal with all possible haste.

A few moments later, Amelia appeared at the far end of the hall. At her side was the piano player.

"She doesn't intend to perform, does she?" Jessie asked Ki.

Amelia, apparently unaware of the deaths, offered a gracious smile to her audience and took her position next to the piano.

"That is most likely," Ki answered. "It is almost a certainty."

Jessie watched Amelia nod to the musician and begin singing. It was not opera that sprang forth from her mouth, but rather an upbeat popular song. Many of the passengers recognized the tune and immediately began smiling their approval.

The effect of the new material was not lost on Amelia. As soon as she saw the smiles, she entered into the second verse with renewed energy. And, when the song was finished, the applause was most enthusiastic.

"Ki, I truly do not give a fiddler's damn what anybody says, people outside of Texas are the strangest bunch I ever saw," Jessie said.

"It would appear that way," Ki replied.

"Come on, we have some talking to do," Jessie said, and walked out onto the deck, Ki following right behind her.

Outside, Jessie leaned against the rail, studying the white splash of water below and the dark outline of the distant trees on the shore. "Tell me, Ki, do these deaths seem strange to you?" she asked, surveying the shoreline.

"They are strange in that they are so easy to explain," Ki answered. "I would question any answer that comes so easily."

"That's exactly what I'm doing, but none of it makes sense," Jessie answered. "None of the others has anything to gain. Quigley, Seacrest, and Delamore, their deaths mean nothing to anyone else on the ship."

"Can we be so sure of that?" Ki asked.

"At this point, I'm not sure of anything, except that someone else is bound to die soon," Jessie replied. "And I'm gonna try to stop it if I can."

★

Chapter 12

Stratton, standing like a statue behind the wheel of the ship, said, "Well, Miss Starbuck, the passengers have all managed to survive the night, I take it?"

"It's still morning," Jessie replied. "Give them until this afternoon and there should be another death or two."

"We make Memphis by dusk," Stratton said. "If they want to die, let them do it on dry land and well away from my ship and crew. It's bad, very bad to have passengers die on a ship. It's bad luck. Bad for the morale of the crew."

"Though it doesn't seem to affect the other passengers adversely," Jessie countered.

"And why should it?" Stratton quipped. "They've paid their fare. They have every intention of seeing their money spent to the last penny."

Jessie stood silently for a long time, watching the shoreline slowly pass. "How is the dressing on that arm?" she asked finally. "I should have a look at it."

"No need, I had Wittick change it this morning," Stratton said. "He compliments you on the excellent job. Said it was first-rate."

Jessie, sensing that something was amiss, asked, "You don't seemed pleased."

"Pleased? Should I be?" Stratton snapped. "I've got three dead men in my food locker and I'm captain of a ship about to be owned by a bank."

"Is that bad, the part about the bank?" Jessie asked.

"Bad? It's the worst news a captain of any vessel can hear," Stratton answered angrily. "Bankers and ships do not mix."

"Yet, the bank owns it, anyway, at least in principle. They own the stock."

"Yes, but they couldn't do as they pleased," Stratton said. "They had to contend with our so-called 'investors.' As soon as they get their grubby banker hands on my ship, they'll load it beyond capacity with cargo and squeeze every penny out of her, trying to make their money back in a year while cutting three or four years off the ship's useful life. That's bad business, but you couldn't tell them that. I've seen it before, Jessie. Ships that I knew were not two years old, looking like ten. Bad business."

The vehemence of Stratton's small speech startled Jessie. Clearly, he was a man whose love of ships was passionate, but more importantly, she felt that she could also rule him out as a suspect in the untimely deaths of the investors.

"If you'll excuse me now, Captain, I believe I'll take some air on the deck," Jessie said.

As she was turning to leave, Stratton summoned the first mate to the wheel. "Jessie, wait," Stratton said as he gave up the wheel.

As she turned back to the bridge, she saw Stratton coming toward her. "I feel I must apologize for that," he said, approaching. "It's just that I see what's in store for this ship, but I won't be a party to what they'll do to her."

"You're resigning?" she asked, a little shocked.

"As soon as we reach New Orleans," he replied. "I don't have a choice. Even if no more of the investors die, the bank is certain to make an offer for the outstanding shares."

Jessie was about to answer something, but before the words could even form themselves in her brain, a cry went up from below. "Man overboard! Man overboard!"

Turning in a flash, Stratton raced back to the bridge as Jessie ran down the stairs to the deck. As soon as she reached the deck, she saw the crowd lined up at the railing, watching in horror as a man's suited arms splashed in the water.

Jessie kicked off her boots and leapt the rail with one hand, then fell the thirty feet to the water. When she hit, it was feetfirst in the churning current. For an instant, she was submerged, and when she resurfaced, her arms were already moving, taking long strokes toward the drowning man.

He was still a hundred feet away as she swam frantically against the current. The same powerful current was also carrying the drowning man toward her. With every stroke she made, the distance between them shrank.

The arms lowered again, splashing, and then he rose, washed upward in the water by the ship's wash. When she was fifty feet away, she could see him, the bald pate, the pale face twisted into a mask of horror. It was Strope!

Someone threw a life preserver from the deck, and Strope struggled toward it. Suddenly, there was a deafening grinding sound and the huge sidewheels came to a halt. Almost immediately the ship began drifting free in the current, turning sideways so that it appeared to block Strope's progress.

When she was nearly to him, the large wooden hull of the ship looming large beside them, Jessie grabbed the life ring and held it in one hand.

Suddenly, just as he came within an arm's reach, Strope vanished, carried under the ship by the current.

In a flash, Jessie pulled the knife from her boot sheath, cut the rope on the preserver, and tied it to her belt. A second later, she was diving. She knew she would need the rope, a lifeline, to pull her back out from under the ship.

Jessie opened her eyes under the ship and could see almost nothing. The water was inky black from the mud and only a few stray columns of light managed to pierce the darkness. Swimming with her arms out, reaching at every stroke, Jessie made her way to the center of the ship. She only hoped that the lifeline was long enough, and her lungs strong enough.

Then she felt him, her fingers grazing along a patch of material, before he drifted out of reach again. Her lungs ready to burst, she kicked out and took a long stroke, but the line yanked her back.

She reached out again and the material touched her hand. Frantically, she grabbed, caught just a small portion of it in her hand. Somehow she managed a firmer grip and pulled. Strope's limp body floated toward her through the water. She pulled again, released her grip, then grabbed what she knew to be his belt.

Kicking and using one arm to stroke, she frantically made her way to the edge of the ship's hull. Above her, whoever was in possession of the other end of the line, felt it go slack. They began pulling mightily, dragging her out from under the ship.

Just as Jessie felt she was about to pass out, she saw the light streaming through the water at the edge of the ship's hull. When she broke the surface, she was gagging and choking. Instantly, two strong pairs of hands, stewards who had jumped in after her, supported her in the water, as another pulled the gasping Strope to the surface.

Looking up, Jessie spotted Ki on the deck, the rope from her life preserver held tightly in his hands, a grim expression on his face.

Two more life preservers appeared, splashing nearby in the water. The stewards fastened one of the rings around Strope and then took the other for themselves. Two other crew members lowered a rope ladder, and Jessie swam gratefully for it, allowing Ki to pull her part of the way.

A few minutes later, Jessie was wrapped in a blanket and sitting in a chair in the salon. Someone was holding a brandy out to her. A large crowd of passengers and crew were gathered around, their faces showing expressions of concern.

"I just wanted to tell you, that was a damned fool thing to do," Stratton said in a low voice, so that only Jessie could hear.

"Where's Strope?" Jessie asked. She had not seen him since they'd pulled him on deck.

"He's back in his cabin. Wittick's attending to him," Stratton said. "I suspect he'll be just fine. Some drunks are lucky that way."

"Did anyone see what happened?" Jessie asked, taking a sip of the brandy.

"No, he was alone on deck," Stratton answered. "He said he was walking along and the next thing he remembered was being in the water."

Jessie waited until the gawkers got tired and wandered off. Then she said, "You mean, he climbed up on the rail and fell in?"

"He's a drunk. Who knows what he did?" Stratton answered. "He might have been looking over the side and lost his balance. Anything could have happened."

"I want to see," Jessie said, rising.

"See what, the rail?"

"Yes," Jessie said, wrapping the blanket around her tightly and walking out on the deck.

Stratton and Ki followed her out as she ran her hand along the polished wood. "The way I figure it, he must have fallen around here," she said, then suddenly came to a stop. "Ki, would you look at this?" she said, her voice low.

Ki stepped around the captain so that he was beside Jessie. Immediately, he saw it, too. The place in the rail was split for a gate, where a gangplank could be fitted.

"I see it," Ki said.

"What? It's a gate," Stratton replied without enthusiasm.

"Watch," Jessie said, and kicked the portion gently. The gate swung open. "He must have fallen through here."

Stratton, clearly dismayed, pulled the portion of rail back. "I don't understand this," he said. "It must be the lock."

The gate was held in place by a simple lever device, which when lifted, allowed it to swing open. The lever was lifted, even though gravity and its own weight should have kept it locked down. Only the fact that the gate was so tightly fitted kept it from being immediately noticeable or from swinging completely free.

"Look at this, Captain," Jessie said, removing a thick wad of newspaper from the lever. "Do you still think those accidents were a matter of bad luck?"

The instant the newspaper was removed, the lever fell closed. "I'll be damned," Stratton whispered.

"Observe also, the door," Ki said.

Jessie and Stratton looked directly behind them to a service door. Whoever had pushed Strope through the gate had an easy means of escape. It would require only a mild push, for Strope was already unsteady on his feet from drink, and then a matter of a step or two into the door. It was, both Jessie and Stratton observed, the perfect getaway.

"Where does that door lead?" Jessie asked.

Stratton shrugged. "The kitchen, the hold, the engine room, even to the passenger and crew cabins," he said. "You could have access to the entire ship through this door."

"May I be so bold as to make a suggestion, Captain?" Ki asked.

"I don't see what harm it could do," Stratton answered.

Ki nodded politely, then said, "I would suggest you confine the remaining investors to their cabins. It appears that whoever is the murderer is only interested in murdering these men. In their cabins there would be little opportunity."

"A fine idea," Stratton said. "Only I don't think they'll sit still for it."

"You must order them to do it," Ki said. "You could do it under the guise of house arrest."

"Won't that get them more riled up?" Jessie asked.

"It would, but at least it would give me the authority," Stratton answered, smiling. "And what do I give a damn? I won't be captain anymore once we reach New Orleans."

Just as the captain was striding off to give the orders to his first mate, Wittick approached them. He was grim-faced as only a doctor could be. "You should be quite proud of yourself, Miss Starbuck," he said. "You saved that man's life."

"How is he?" Jessie asked.

Wittick's frown deepened. "He's barely aware of what happened," he said. "Still drunk as a lord. As a matter of fact, I suspect you couldn't be able to guess what he's doing at this moment."

"Drinking?" Jessie ventured.

"That goes without saying," Wittick replied. "No, he's taking a bath. He believes that it will be effective in eliminating the chill."

"You would think he has had enough water for one day," Jessie said. "I certainly have."

"Yes, you would suppose so," Wittick answered. "However, for you, I would prescribe a fresh change of clothes, immediately."

"You know, I just think I'll take that advice," Jessie said, and headed for her cabin.

★

Chapter 13

They reached Memphis just after nightfall. As they approached the dock, Jessie and Ki could see the crowds gathered under the light of the lanterns.

"Looks like a big turnout," Jessie said, as the large ship maneuvered into the dock.

"Why shouldn't it be?" a man standing at the rail next to Jessie said. "It isn't every day that a new ship pulls in and unloads three dead rich men. Hell, that's something I might even show up to see."

Jessie had to admit that the gentleman had a point. No doubt the notoriety of the ship was spread by newspaper and telegraph. The men who they left behind to search for Quigley's body had doubtless spread the word.

As the gangplank was lowered and the passengers disembarked, a murmur went up through the crowd. Newspapermen surrounded the passengers, eager for an account of the tragedies, which the passengers were only too eager to provide.

Just as the last of the passengers were stepping down the gangplank, Stratton and his first mate approached Jessie. "Have you by any chance seen Strope?" he asked.

"Not since this afternoon," Jessie replied. "He's probably sleeping."

"I think we better investigate," Stratton said. "I have a bad feeling about this."

Jessie and Ki followed Stratton down the main corridor to the luxury passenger cabins. Knocking on the door, Stratton called, "Mr. Strope, we've arrived in Memphis!"

No answer came from inside.

"Mr. Strope!" Stratton called again.

Jessie, impatient with the yelling, tried the door. The gold-plated handle lifted easily and the door opened. The four of them hesitated, then Jessie walked in. Stratton, Ki, and the first mate followed right behind.

What the four saw brought them up short. There, in the center of the cabin, was Strope's enamel-and-gold bathing tub filled with water. Emerging just above the top of the cold water, like a sandbar, was the shining pate of Strope. The remainder of his head, up to just above his eyebrows, was submerged. A generously filled brandy snifter was still wedged between his fingers. He had drowned in his bathtub.

"It would appear that you're a bit late to pull

him out of that water, Miss Starbuck," Stratton said.

"At least he managed to die clean," the first mate mumbled.

"This wasn't an accident," Jessie declared. "I don't give a damn how it looks. This wasn't an accident."

"You know, I am deeply and sincerely inclined to believe you, Miss Starbuck," Stratton said.

"You better call the doctor," Jessie said, turning on her heel and leaving the room.

"Where are you going?" Stratton asked, anxious.

"I'm going to find myself a decent hotel," Jessie said. "I've had just about as much as I can stand of this floating graveyard."

Jessie stormed out of the room, Ki right at her heels. He, too, was tired of the ship. When she reached the deck, she noticed that the crowds on the docks had thinned out substantially, a fact that she assumed was due to the removal of the bodies. No doubt, the loading of fuel and unloading of cargo held little interest for the residents of Memphis.

Stempley, standing at the rail, stepped into the center of the deck when he noticed Jessie and Ki's approach. "My dear girl, where are you off to in such a hurry?" he asked, his mood lightened considerably.

"Off to a hotel for the night," Jessie answered, her progress off the boat blocked by the old man.

"Excellent idea," Stempley said. "If I may make a recommendation, I just happen to have an address here." He began searching his pockets for the address of a hotel. Presently, he extracted a small slip of paper and handed it to Jessie.

"Thank you. Now, you must excuse me," she said.

"You won't be disappointed," Stempley said. "The others and I had counted on staying at the same hotel. I'll bet you old Strope will have flowers sent to your room. After all, it's not every day a beautiful woman saves your life."

"I doubt it," Jessie said, anxiously pushing past Stempley.

"No, I wouldn't be surprised, not one bit," the old man answered. "Why, just as soon as he sobers up enough to realize what happened—"

"He's not going to sober up," Jessie called over her shoulder. "He's dead."

"What? What? That's impossible!" Stempley said. "Why, I—"

Before he had time to form the remainder of his thought and give it voice, Jessie was already down the gangplank and out of hearing.

When Jessie finally set her feet on dry land, she could feel herself breath a sigh of relief. "Now, where the hell is a carriage?" she asked Ki.

"I do not think it was wise to walk away from Mr. Stempley like you did," Ki said.

"Ki, you're right," Jessie replied. "I just couldn't stand that damned boat anymore. Not a second longer."

"He is not the enemy," Ki said. "The enemy is someone else. And we should find him."

Jessie spotted a long line of carriages for hire

along the street and began walking quickly for them. "I know, you're right," she answered, "but it's just too damned complicated."

"It is not complicated," Ki said. "It is about greed, and greed is not complicated."

Jessie reached the first carriage in line and climbed in, just as a gent was climbing in from the opposite side. She was about to say something when she noticed it was Givens, the gambler.

"Good day to you, Miss Starbuck," Givens said, climbing into the carriage.

"I thought you were confined to your cabin," Jessie said.

"Climb in, Jessie, Ki," Givens invited. "Plenty of room for all three. Climb in and I'll tell you what led to my fortuitous release."

Jessie and Ki climbed in, if for no other reason than to keep an eye on Givens. Jessie was about to hand the slip of paper that Stempley provided to the driver, when Givens smoothly snatched it out of her hand. "Do you mind, Mr. Givens?" she asked.

"Not at all, an excellent hotel," he said, studying the slip of paper before passing it along to the coachman. "An excellent choice, and by coincidence, the very hotel I myself was about to seek lodging in."

They had progressed for some time down the cobblestone streets in uncomfortable silence before Jessie said, "Now, how did you leave your cabin, if I may be so bold as to ask?"

"Very simply, I just left," Givens said. "With the whole crew racing about, I thought it presented an unpardonable inconvenience for me to linger longer than necessary."

"So, you just walked off?" Jessie asked.

"In a manner of speaking," Givens answered. "In all frankness, I would seriously doubt that they will miss my absence, even now."

"Perhaps not the crew, but I would say that the local authorities might find your departure—how would you say it—premature."

"Perhaps, but the local authorities, such as they are, are bound by formalities," Givens said. "A few answers, a few questions, and some other tedious matters, and I'd be in the carriage off to a fine hotel just as we are now. Nothing at all would change. Nothing."

"You seem mighty confident in your case," Jessie replied.

"Why shouldn't I be confident?" he answered. "I am innocent of Mr. Delamore's unfortunate demise."

"You shot him in front of witnesses, a marked deck of cards on the floor, and a great deal of his money in your pocket," Jessie noted. "I would not call the circumstances those in which an innocent man might find himself."

"Details, all of them details," Givens said.

"Details that could hang you," Jessie countered.

Givens was uncharacteristically silent for a long time. Finally he said, "I am innocent. I would trust in your intelligence to think me innocent as well."

It was true. Jessie had to admit, if just to

herself, that she knew Givens did not cheat at cards. Coupled with that fact, she had every reason to believe that the marked cards found at the scene had been placed there when Givens and Delamore were in the dining room. If the murderer could place marked cards around the table, then why not a faulty cartridge in Delamore's pistol? Whoever had accomplished these things had sealed Delamore's fate just as surely as if he had shot the man himself.

"What do you want from me?" Jessie asked. "It was not an accident that you came to this carriage, was it?"

"Again, that fierce intelligence at work," Givens said. "No, I was waiting for you."

"Why?" Jessie replied.

"Why? Because I need your help in clearing my good name," Givens answered. "Even if I am quietly cleared on this charge by the police, there is still the other matter of my reputation. My reputation is my strongest asset. If even the smallest doubt remains, I cannot work on the river again. For a man in my position, the consequences of that would be devastating."

"You mean to tell me that you might have to find honest work?" Jessie asked.

"Banish the thought! Even the most honorable of work is just a stone's throw from manual labor," Givens said, nearly outraged. "What it means is that I'd be forced to head east to ply my trade on the European ships. I have done that, Miss Starbuck, in my foolish youth. There is no joy in it."

"You mean you are forced to look at the people you win from for weeks at a time?" she asked. "On the river you can leave a boat in a matter of days, at the most. Isn't that right?"

Givens smiled his acknowledgement that Jessie was indeed correct in this assumption, then said, "Driver, please, stop here."

A moment later, the carriage came to a halt. They were still a good distance from the hotel. "Aren't you going to the hotel?" Jessie asked.

"Me? I would be a fool to show my face there," he said. "In a very short while, they will discover me missing."

Givens climbed down from the carriage, then paid the coachman.

"How do you need me to help?" Jessie asked.

"Do this," Givens instructed. "Find out all you can of the murders. I will do the same. We will meet tomorrow, and see if we can't catch this rascal."

"Where will you be staying, which hotel?" Jessie asked.

Givens smiled again, this time at Jessie's crude attempt to gain information. "I wouldn't ask you to trouble yourself," he said. "I'll contact you, though, at my convenience. Good day."

Quickly, Givens vanished into an alleyway and was gone. A moment later, the carriage was moving through the darkened streets toward the hotel.

"He is a very strange man," Jessie said, turning to Ki.

"Yes, he is very strange," Ki answered. "I suspect he is well suited to his work."

"Do you think he did it?" Jessie asked.

"We know he shot Mr. Delamore," Ki said. "Though I do not think he cheated. I do not think he needed to cheat a man like Delamore."

"So, you think we should trust him?"

"No, I do not think that we should trust him," Ki answered, "but I think we should help him."

They rode the remainder of the way in silence. When they pulled up in front of the hotel, Stempley was smoking a large cigar and pacing up and down in front. Apparently, Givens's conversation had taken longer than Jessie thought.

"Jessie, I can't tell you how glad I am that you're here," Stempley said, edging the doorman out of the way to help her down. "That rogue has escaped!"

"Who? What rogue?" she asked, already knowing the answer.

"That cheat and murderer, Givens," Stempley answered. "He got off the ship somehow and has made good his escape."

For a split second, Jessie thought of telling Stempley of her encounter with Givens, then thought better of it. "Why, that's a shame," she said.

★

Chapter 14

Jessie, having rested in her room, entered the hotel dining room to find Moran and Stempley engaged in a heated discussion. The dinner plates had been cleared away and each had an untouched snifter of brandy in front of him. Two forgotten cigars were in the process of turning to ash at their elbows.

As Jessie approached the table, the conversation came to an abrupt halt. "Don't let me interrupt," Jessie said, seating herself at the table without an invitation.

"Miss Starbuck, this is hardly the time for a social call," Moran said. "Even by a lady so beautiful."

"Is there a problem?" Jessie asked, feigning ignorance. Although the men could be engaged in a discussion over the untimely deaths of their friends and fellow investors, she doubted it. More than likely, they were talking about money.

"Please, Jessie, this is important," Stempley said.

"Is it more important than murder?" she answered back.

"Damn right, you're damned right it's more important than murder," Moran said.

"And just what is more important?" Jessie asked, already knowing the answer.

"Money," Moran said. "A great deal of money."

The answer didn't shock Jessie, though she didn't expect to hear it expressed quite so bluntly. "I see," was all she managed as answer.

"I've just received this telegraph," Stempley explained, indicating the yellow sheet of paper spread out across the table. "It's from the bank in St. Louis. They've made us a very generous offer for our remaining shares of the ship."

"Generous? Like hell it's generous!" Moran spat. "Those damn bankers are trying to steal her! Do you hear what I'm telling you? They are trying to steal our damned boat."

"Nevertheless, it's quite generous, under the circumstances," Stempley insisted. "Under the circumstances, we must entertain it."

"The only thing I'll entertain is giving those banker sons of bitches a kick in the pants!" Moran spat. "A week ago I'd have spit in their faces. And you would have, too."

"But now?" Jessie asked.

"Now isn't a week ago," Stempley sadly conceded. "Now is now, and we've had several unfortunate setbacks."

"The murders," Jessie stated.

"The murders, of course, they play a part in this whole sad tragedy. We have become unable to book passengers on the ship," Stempley said. "It's the passengers who pay the way. The costs of crew, fuel, maintenance, and taxes were all paid by passengers. The cargo was where we expected to earn our profits."

"And now the passengers we have are demanding their money back," Moran continued. "And nobody wants to ship freight on her. It's a damned mess."

"I say we consider this offer the bank's made," Stempley sighed. "I say we consider the offer with the utmost seriousness."

"How much is it for?" Jessie asked.

"Half," Moran stated, his voice filled with disgust. "They are offering us half of what our shares in the ship are worth. It's half, right down to the last penny."

"There is an alternative," Jessie said. "You could offer to buy their shares for the same amount."

"What?" Moran blurted out, nearly overturning both his brandy and cigar.

"Spend our own money?" Stempley added. "Jessie, I've known you for a long time. I must confess, I always thought you had a better head for business than that."

"I have a fine head for business," Jessie answered. "I inherited it from my father and, as I recall, you and he were friends once."

"That we were," Stempley answered, his mood softening at Jessie's mention of her dead father.

"What do you suppose he would think of all this fanciness about using a bank's money?" Jessie asked. "What do you suppose he'd say to you?"

"Jessie, things have changed," Stempley replied. "A great many things have changed since your father and I started together in Texas."

"The only thing that's changed is you," Jessie replied firmly. "You've grown soft and lazy. You're afraid you might have to do without those cigars and brandy."

"I've grown old, Jessie. I'm an old man now, in case you haven't noticed."

Jessie, disgusted, got up to leave. "Old, yes, but old doesn't mean soft, weak, and afraid," Jessie answered. "Where I grew up, old meant smart, even wise, not tricky. The way I see it, you've got nothing to complain about if you've been out-tricked by bankers."

With that, Jessie left. As she walked from the table, she heard Moran say, "Women don't have the brains for business. It just isn't in them."

Stempley made no comment to this.

So intent was Jessie on leaving the dining room and getting away from Stempley and Moran, that she didn't see Stratton striding in. The two collided, Jessie nearly toppling over backward.

"Oh, excuse me, I—" Stratton started, then saw it was Jessie. He, too, had been distracted. "Jessie, what are you doing here?"

"The better question is, why aren't you with your precious ship?" she countered.

The captain hesitated a moment, then said, "I'm offering my resignation. I can't wait until New

130

Orleans. The faster I get away from that ship, the better."

"Well, you're probably offering it to the wrong two men," Jessie snapped.

Stratton's face clouded over with confusion. Clearly that was Stempley and Moran in the dining room beyond. If those weren't the correct two men, then who were? Did Jessie mean that he should hand his meticulously written letter of resignation to one or all of the three dead men carried off the ship?

"They're about to sell the ship to the bankers," Jessie said to clear up the captain's obvious confusion. "Probably, they're just deciding on a price now, or if they can get the bankers to raise their offer."

"I knew it!" Stratton blurted out. "I knew it was just a matter of time before they turned coward."

"You're a fine one to be talking about cowards," Jessie replied. "I'd say that you could teach those two something about being cowards."

"I won't captain a vessel owned by bankers," Stratton replied. "Even a fine ship like that one. It just isn't worth it."

"Well, go ahead then, hand them that letter," Jessie answered and began walking away.

Stratton immediately began to follow her across the hotel lobby. "Don't you see? I don't have a choice," he pleaded. "I just don't have a choice."

"Yes, you do," Jessie said, without turning, then headed up the wide staircase that led to her room.

Stratton followed, hot on her heels. "What? What choice do I have?"

"Help me find the person who did it," she said.

"You know who did it?" Stratton asked. "You know who killed those men?"

"Not yet," Jessie answered. "But I will. And when I do find the culprit, he's going to wish he'd never seen a river. Any river and any boat."

They reached the top of the stairs together, Stratton walking briskly alongside Jessie. "Do you have a plan?" he asked.

"Something like a plan," she said. "I have an idea of one, anyway."

"But you're not going to tell me, right?"

"Not yet," she answered. "Can I count on your help?"

"You can if it keeps the ship out of the hands of the damned bankers," Stratton answered. "And—"

"And what?" Jessie said, stopping suddenly in the corridor.

"And, if it gets me into your room," Stratton added.

Jessie turned, the key to her room already in her hand. "What's more important to you? Catching the killer or killers and keeping the ship out of the hands of bankers, or—"

"Getting into your room?" Stratton finished.

"Yes."

"I would answer that we should take first things first," Stratton replied, then leaned down and kissed her.

As the strong arms of the captain embraced her, Jessie lost all resolve to argue. Instinctively, she knew she could count on him. She knew,

132

somehow, that he'd lay down his life for her, if not the ship. And that was all she needed to know, for the moment anyway. If the truth be told, she was more interested in getting him inside her room than saving the ship from bankers at that very moment.

As their lips touched, she felt the excitement surge through her. As the passion of the kiss flowed through her, Jessie felt her knees slowly give way and nearly her full weight press into Stratton. He supported her effortlessly, his strong arms wrapped deliciously around her.

Very slowly then, still kissing, the captain released one arm from around her waist and took the room key from Jessie's hand. Without fumbling, he slid the key into the lock and gently kicked the door open.

When he took her again in both arms, it was with renewed strength that lifted her booted feet from the carpet. As she wrapped her legs around his waist, he easily carried her into the room as if she weighed no more than a feather, and then kicked the door closed behind them.

Still kissing, Stratton carried her to the bed and gently released her to the thick, soft embrace of the feather mattress. Then he was beside her, kissing her lips once again, before his own lips began straying down the smooth curve of her neck.

Jessie, suddenly blushing, realized that she had dressed that day without undergarments, then abandoned the thought as her mind turned to the amorous pleasure the good captain was offering her with his lips.

Slowly he worked his way down her neck with his lips, until, finally, he was at that point where her shirt buttoned at the throat. Unfastening the first button, he noted the spot with a lingering kiss. He did the same for the second, third, and fourth buttons as his warm, full lips dallied and played across her smooth skin.

When he reached the point where the womanly curve of her breast was exposed under the shirt, he paused, a little surprised, then began again, greedy and thankful that she was indeed not wearing undergarments.

When her shirt was completely opened, he moved his head between her breasts, inhaling her womanly scent deeply. Then, lifting one full, firm breast with his hand, he turned his head slightly and began kissing the sensitive place around her nipple, letting his lips wander slowly toward the center.

Jessie sighed in passion, then managed, through a well-practiced maneuver to pry off first one boot, then the other.

Stratton reluctantly lifted his mouth from her nipple, tingling in the cool air, and began kissing the other, drawing it gently between his lips, where his tongue could toy with it.

After a long time, he abandoned the second nipple as well, leaving it firm, hard, and tingling deliciously as he moved his mouth down her smooth, flat stomach. When he reached her belt buckle, he stopped. Then, opening her belt and trousers with one hand, continued his downward journey.

Jessie lifted her hips slowly, just long enough for him to pull her trousers off, and again, he was pleasantly surprised at her lack of undergarments.

Standing at the foot of the bed, Stratton quickly undressed as Jessie watched, her eyes blazing with passion. Then, spreading her long, graceful legs wide, she invited him to her, as he returned to the bed.

"Please, now, don't wait," Jessie moaned, as she felt the hot length of his shaft brush against her thigh.

The captain was all too pleased to yield to her wishes. Fumbling just a little awkwardly, he guided himself into her, feeling the moist heat surge through him.

Jessie raised her hips, meeting the first long, slow, steady stroke of his shaft that filled her. When he was completely inside, he paused, just for a moment, then began to pull away. Inch by inch, the long, hard member withdrew until it was nearly completely out of her, then slowly, he lowered himself, once again filling her.

Soon he was moving back and forth, his hard member sliding easily in and out of Jessie's moist womanhood. Once again he busied himself with her breasts, sliding the open shirt down over the milky white shoulders, so that he could kiss his way to their center.

With each kiss, he lingered just a little longer, until once again, his lips were teasing and pulling at her ripe, pink nipples.

Soon, Jessie could contain herself no longer. Reaching around his back, she pulled him into her, clutching at his firm backside, forcing him deeper and deeper into her as her body convulsed with pleasure.

Again and again the great waves of sensuous pleasure washed over her, touching every muscle in her body, until finally she was calling out, her fingers raking along the skin of his back. Her hips raised and bucked, and she wrapped her long legs around him, forcing him deeper and shortening his sure strokes.

When she was spent and sweat-covered, she reached down and gently guided him out of her. Then, still holding his member, she pulled him up, so that now he was kneeling above her, his thick shaft inches from her mouth.

Raising her head slightly, she took just the tip of his shaft into her mouth, and using her hands, brought her breasts up so that they encased it on either side.

Slowly and tentatively at first, Stratton began moving his hips so that the shaft moved gently in and out of her mouth and between her breasts. Jessie raised her head again and took as much of the shaft into her mouth as she could.

In a short time, he was pumping with long regular strokes, the member moving hotly, wetly, between her firm, full breasts and her mouth. And then he had reached his moment, the hot stream surged into her, and she gulped at it greedily.

When he was finished, Jessie held the shaft between her breasts for a long time, listening to the captain's breathing return to normal.

Presently, he rolled off, taking a position next to her and bending his head to kiss her. "Was that part of your plan?" he asked, wrapping his arm around her.

Jessie settled into the crook of his arm, feeling comfort in his well-muscled body. "That was part of my plan," she said, a sly grin breaking out over her face.

"If that's the way it begins, then I can't wait for the way it ends," he answered.

"Listen, I have to tell you something," Jessie said, her voice changing its tone so that the captain could make no mistake that she was serious.

"And what would that be?" he asked, pulling her closer and leaning just a little into her.

"I've seen Givens," she said. "And he wants to help us find out who did the killing."

"Givens? That son of a bitch, I don't need any help from the likes of him," Stratton said, his entire body suddenly going tense.

"The way I see it, we don't have much of a choice," Jessie answered. "He's offered to help, and I think we should take him up on it."

"And just what's in it for him?" Stratton asked. "I know his type; he won't do anything unless it benefits him."

"He thinks it will help him clear his name," Jessie replied.

"Nothing will ever clear his name," came the answer. "That miserable cur—"

But before Stratton could finish, all hell seemed to break loose. From out in the hall came the

sounds of a woman screaming. Doors began opening and slamming. Soon, a chorus of men's voices
was added to the screaming, and a dozen footsteps
sounded in the hall.

★

Chapter 15

Jessie and Stratton rolled from the bed. Throwing their clothes on in extreme haste, they ran to the door, collided, then bolted into the hallway. Out in the wide hall of the hotel was a young woman, dressed in nothing more than a pair of stockings and shoes. She was screaming incomprehensibly at the center of a group of men, none of whom were doing anything to either help or even to dress her for that matter.

She was a beautiful woman with a full head of thick, red curls and large breasts. Jessie noted that her face was painted just a little too vividly to be a guest. She had seen such faces painted on women in New York, San Francisco, and elsewhere. It was, she knew, the face of a prostitute.

For their part, the men seemed to treat the entire affair as something of a pleasurable joke— an evening's unusual diversion. It was impossible to understand what the woman was screaming, and in truth, they didn't much care.

Finally, Ki came through the crowd, and offered the young, nearly naked woman a blanket. She looked at the blanket uncomprehendingly at first, then snatched it from Ki and continued shouting her story, this time making a little more sense than before. "He's dead! He's dead!" the young woman chanted over and over, appealing to first one man, then another, not standing still long enough for any of them to question her.

"Who? Who is dead?" Ki asked, halting the woman's progress around the circle of men by grabbing her arms.

At this point several of the men appeared to regain their senses sufficiently enough to treat the episode with some measure of seriousness.

"The gent in the room!" the young redheaded woman cried. "We were in bed and he just . . . just died!"

"What room?" Ki demanded, shaking the girl slightly, trying to force her back to her senses.

"I've heard about these things," the woman said. "I heard about them, but I never thought—never thought I would be a party to it! I didn't kill him, he did it all himself!"

"Which room? Where is the dead man?" Ki demanded again.

"We were in bed," the woman said. "The gent in the lobby sent me up to him, like a gift, I guess. And we were in bed and he died! But I didn't kill nobody. I didn't kill him. He did it all himself, he did!"

"Which room?" Ki shouted. "Tell me!"

At this point, the woman seemed to collapse, all the fight draining out of her. "Two hundred five," she said.

Ki released her and ran down the hall, followed by the other members of the mob, which by now numbered some twenty-five or more people, including Jessie and Stratton.

Ki pushed through the room and into the sitting room, followed by the others. Off to one side of the room he found the door to the bedroom. The crowd surged forward in the small sitting room, pushing at the bedroom door. When Ki finally managed to open it, they let out a collective gasp.

There, propped up in bed, naked, was Moran. The color was drained from his face, though Jessie thought she detected just the hint of a smile.

Coming forward, pushing his way through the crowd, Stratton put two fingers to Moran's neck to feel for a pulse. "Well, she was damned right," the captain said. "He's dead."

"One helluva way to go out," someone in the crowd said. His pronouncement was met by nervous chuckles.

Stratton closed Moran's eyes, then turned on the crowd. "The lot of you now, get the hell outta here! Give the man some common respect."

The crowd began to quit the room slowly. As Jessie turned to leave, she searched the crowd for the redheaded woman, but she was nowhere in sight.

Edging her way through the mumbling crowd, she broke back into the hall. It was empty. The

141

redheaded woman had vanished, probably forever, into the Memphis night.

Jessie went back to the room and began to straighten her disheveled clothes. A few seconds later, she was joined by Stratton. "Well, he's dead all right," he said. "The hotel doctor just made it official. He probably died of a heart attack."

"The woman disappeared," Jessie replied, slipping her boots back on. "I can't say that I blame her, but it doesn't make things any easier. Did you hear what she said? It was something about a man sending her up to the room."

"I know," Stratton answered. "Did you know that Moran was under strict orders from his doctor to avoid exertion of any kind? When the doctor told him that, it just about broke his heart. He fancied himself a real ladies' man."

"Who knew that?" Jessie asked, standing up to tuck her shirttail in.

"Counting you and me?" Stratton replied, buttoning his shirt.

Jessie nodded as answer.

"Probably not more than two or three hundred people, counting everyone on the boat."

"That seems unlikely," Jessie replied. "That seems highly unlikely."

"There was some speculation, when we began, that he might try to smuggle a young woman on the boat disguised as a passenger," Stratton answered. "Failing that, there was always the chance that he'd somehow manage to seduce one of the other passenger's wives."

Jessie waited, listening in disbelief.

"Wittick thought it wise to circulate the rumor that Moran had a weak heart among the passengers," Stratton continued. "If it was known, then the chances of just such an occurrence would be greatly reduced."

Jessie though on it for a moment. Then she remembered that when Moran approached her, he had said something about a weak heart. He'd probably mentioned it to save himself any sort of embarrassment. "Well, then you'd agree that he was killed," Jessie said. "Whoever sent that woman up to his room intended to murder him. You'll agree with that assumption, won't you?"

Stratton thought on it for a moment, then answered, "I don't think that they meant him any good. But I don't see how you could call it murder. I mean, what would the charge be? It isn't like shooting someone."

"Or poisoning, or drowning, or even engineering a duel," Jessie continued. "But whatever you want to call it, whatever name you want to put on it, it's still intended to gain the same thing."

"To hand the ship over to the bankers," Stratton concluded.

Just then, there was a soft knock at the door. It was a knock that Jessie had heard enough in her lifetime to know it could belong to nobody but Ki. Without asking who was there, she rose, crossed the room, and opened the door. Standing in the hall was Ki. Standing directly behind him, looking a little sheepish, was Amelia.

"Moran is dead," Ki said.

"I know," Jessie replied. "Now all we have to find out is who did it."

"I know who did it, Miss Starbuck," Amelia said anxiously. "I know who did it."

Stratton was off the bed and at the door in a flash, pulling Ki and Amelia into the room. "Who did it?" he demanded, facing Amelia. "Who was it?"

"It was that girl," Amelia said. "The one in the hall."

Stratton's face turned sour, disgusted. "Not her! I know that!"

"No, I meant to say, I know that girl," Amelia said. "I mean, I used to know her. I mean before she started to, you know. Her name is Annie Wengro. We worked at the same saloon a few years ago."

"Well, that does us no good," he answered. "Who cares if you know her?"

"She knows where the girl lives," Ki offered. "Perhaps if we could find her—"

"She'll tell us who sent her up to the room," Jessie concluded.

"Or at least be able to describe him," Ki said.

"Can you take us there?" Stratton asked, his tone softening.

"It's in a bad part of town. Decent folks don't go there much," Amelia said. "I mean—"

"Let's go," Stratton replied curtly, nearly already out the door.

Jessie, Ki, and Amelia followed Stratton, who seemed to know where he was going. By the time they reached the front entrance of the hotel, however, he'd slowed up considerably, faced with the necessity of Amelia's directions.

It took them some time, but the four finally managed to hire a carriage to take them to the young woman's home. None of the very few carriages waiting outside wanted to travel that far or into that area late at night. Finally, they found a stout-hearted driver who would make the journey for double the usual price.

"I remember Annie from when I sang here in Memphis in the old days," Amelia said. "That was before I went to New York to study opera. She always wanted to be an actress."

"What happened?" Jessie asked, mildly curious to hear the story.

"There was a rich man," Amelia said. "Then there was another rich man. They both promised to take her to New York, but never did. Then there was a not-so-rich man. And then two not-so-rich men. I guess it's like arithmetic. Pretty soon none of the men were very rich. I guess by then it didn't matter very much to her. But she was a very nice person. She used to make me laugh. When I last saw her, she made me cry."

Nobody said anything. The horses' hooves echoed lonely on the cobblestones as the houses changed from opulent to not-so-opulent, and then to shabby. The streets became more and more narrow.

Toward the end of the trip, Amelia had to tell the driver where to turn. It wasn't often that he took passengers into this part of town, day or night.

When Amelia finally told the driver to stop and Stratton had paid him, they could hear the horses moving quickly along the street.

"It's down this alley," Amelia said. "He wouldn't have been able to come down there."

They followed her down the trash-filled alley. Hidden deep in the piles of refuse and split barrels, rats rustled and scampered.

"Helluva place," Stratton muttered as they continued on their way.

"This is it," Amelia said, stopping suddenly at a crude door.

Jessie, her hand on her Colt, walked up and knocked on the door.

Nobody answered, but inside there was the sound of someone moving about.

Jessie knocked again and the sound ceased.

"Annie, it's me, Amelia!"

No one answered.

Jessie tried the door, pushing it cautiously open with one hand, the other ready with the pistol at her side.

Inside the small room a small lamp burned. Its wick was lowered so that it cast distorted shadows across the walls.

"Annie!" Amelia called again.

Then Jessie saw it. Slumped in the corner at the far end of the room was the redheaded woman. Someone had cut her throat.

"Oh no, they've killed her!" Amelia cried, running to the dead woman.

Just as Amelia began running, there was the sound of footsteps from the adjoining room, then the sound of a door opening.

Jessie drew her gun and followed the sound into the second room, which was a small kitchen. At the far end of the room, the door swung open. Someone was running down the alley.

★

Chapter 16

Jessie approached the corner of the building at a full run. Just as she cleared the edge, a board struck out, catching her full in the stomach. The sudden jolt knocked the gun from her hand, sending her to the ground.

She hit the ground with her left hand breaking the fall, then spun out in the kick that caught her assailant across the knees. He cursed, began to fall, then caught himself against the wall, as Jessie regained her feet. A second later, she lashed out with another kick, a spinning roundhouse. Her boot heel sank deep into his gut, knocking him free of the wall and sending him tumbling into a trash heap.

A moment later, Amelia, Stratton, and Ki were rounding the corner. Jessie walked over and pulled up the gasping man by his shirt front. Even in the dim light of the alley, she could see it was Givens.

"You bastard! It was you all along!" Stratton yelled.

Givens held both hands up in an attitude of defeat, but Stratton was having none of it. Stepping forward next to Jessie, the captain punched Givens so powerfully in the face that he was dislodged from Jessie's grip and fell back into the trash.

A rat, disturbed by the commotion, pried his way up from the refuse and scampered across the gambler's lap. At the sudden movement of the rodent, Givens sprang up partway and crawled painfully on his hands and knees away from the trash.

"You, you, you killed Annie!" Amelia cried. Beside herself with anger, she ran up to deliver a solid kick to Givens's midsection. The blow was harder than Jessie would have thought it could be. It knocked the man over on his back.

"No more, please," he begged, his hands once again up in an attitude of surrender. Then, looking directly at Ki, he asked, "You—you're a rational man, you're not going to hit me, are you?"

"No, I will not hit you," Ki answered flatly.

By this time, Jessie had retrieved her Colt and was holding it on Givens. "Why? What did you have to gain?" she asked.

"Nothing," Givens answered painfully as he tried to get to his feet. "I didn't kill them. None of them."

"You killed Annie!" Amelia yelled.

"I didn't kill anybody," Givens insisted. "I heard about Annie from the hotel manager, who owes me some money. He knew her. I swear, I arrived only just before you people did."

"And you expect us to believe that?" Stratton sneered.

"Believe what you want, it's the truth," Givens answered, swaying slightly on his feet. "I think she broke one of my ribs."

"Prove it," Jessie said.

"Prove it? I can prove it," came the answer. "But we have to go back in there."

A minute later, they were back in the shabby room. Givens, moving slowly under threat of Jessie's Colt, walked to the small lamp and turned the wick up, casting the room in bright yellowish light. "Look, she's had her throat slit, poor girl," he said, motioning to the corpse.

"You're capable of it," Stratton said. "I know your type, you're more than capable of slitting some poor whore's throat, or anybody else's for that matter."

"Maybe I am," Givens answered. "Maybe any of us in this room is capable of it, but not without a knife."

The four of them looked at Givens questioningly.

"Where's the knife?" the gambler said at last. "Where is the knife that slit her throat? Search me if you like. You won't find it."

"I think I'll do that," Stratton said, stepping forward.

Givens let himself be thoroughly and roughly

searched. No knife was produced.

"Now, search the room," Givens challenged. "That's what I was doing when you came in. There is no knife."

"What if we believe you?" Jessie asked. "What then?"

"Miss Starbuck, you have no choice but to believe me," Givens replied, some of his former manner returning as the pain subsided. "Indeed, you have to believe me, as a logical and thoughtful person."

"Just suppose we do believe that you didn't kill this girl," Stratton said. "That doesn't mean that you didn't kill the others."

"Of course it does," Givens said. "What it means, Captain, is that I'm trying to do the same thing that you people are, though admittedly, for different reasons. It also means that we are very close. Another few minutes and we would have had our man."

"I just thought of something," Jessie broke in. "With only one investor left, Stempley's in danger."

"We should get back to the hotel," Stratton said. "We should get back there fast."

"What about Annie? We just can't leave her here," Amelia pleaded. "We can't leave her here like this."

"The dear girl is right," Givens said.

"Ki, you wait here with Amelia," Jessie said. "When we get back to the hotel, we'll find the police."

"Yes, that would probably be best," Ki said.

Amelia didn't think too much of the idea, but conceded that it was the only plan that made sense.

"As for me, I must find my way to the telegraph," Givens said. "I must contact a pair of newspaper friends of mine in New York and Boston."

"Do you mind telling me what in hell a New York or Boston newspaperman would know about these murders?" Stratton asked, annoyed.

"Nothing, nothing whatsoever," Givens answered. "These men, by trade, would not write about a murder if it were presented to them on a silver platter with singing waiters."

"Then what do they write about?" Stratton asked, his annoyance growing.

"Society columns," Givens replied, already halfway out the door. "They write the society columns. Good night!"

"That Givens, I don't like him," Stratton said, as they walked toward a main thoroughfare. "Not one bit."

"But you don't think he's the killer, do you?" Jessie asked.

"No, truthfully, I don't," Stratton answered. "But I hate him just enough so that I wish he were."

Outside a seedy saloon, they found a carriage willing to take them back to the hotel. Like the saloon, the carriage and horse were shabby, but it didn't matter. For an extra fee the driver hurried the horse along the streets to the hotel.

Jessie and Stratton ran from the carriage

directly into the deserted lobby of the hotel. They paused only long enough at the desk to obtain Stempley's room number and to inform the manager to summon the police to the address where they had left Amelia and Ki. Then they flew up the stairs to the second floor.

Jessie began pounding on the door as soon as she reached it. She kept up the pounding for a full half minute. When no answer came from inside, Stratton took a step back, preparing himself to kick it in.

It was just as Stratton was about to launch his attack on the door that Stempley, groggy and wearing his nightshirt, opened the door. "Good lord, what on earth are you two doing?" he asked.

"We were worried about you," Jessie answered somewhat sheepishly.

"With two lunatics trying to break down my hotel room door in the middle of the night, I'm worried about me," came the answer.

"The girl, the one that gave Moran the heart attack, was killed tonight," Stratton said, stepping into the room.

"Murdered?" Stempley asked, stepping aside so Jessie could enter the room.

"Her throat was slit," Jessie said. "Ki and Amelia are there now, waiting for the authorities."

"Frightful business," Stempley said, closing the door and retreating to a nearby chair. "Horrible! I'll be glad to be out of it."

"So you are selling your shares?" Stratton asked.

"I've already wired the bank," Stempley said. "I received the answer just a short time ago. By coincidence, they have a representative traveling through on the way to New Orleans. He'll be able to draw up the final papers."

"I never thought you were a coward," Jessie said.

"Is that what I am now?" came the answer. "A few hours ago I was just another no-good businessman. Now I'm a coward. Honestly, I don't know if I've risen in your estimation or not. Perhaps you'd care to enlighten me."

"You haven't," Jessie said. "Now you're running out to save your skin and your money. You've dropped lower as far as I'm concerned."

"And just what would you suggest I do, young lady?" Stempley asked.

"Wait until tomorrow evening," Jessie said. "Stall them until tomorrow evening."

"And then what?" came the reply.

"Then we'll see," Jessie said. "Either you'll be dead or we'll know who's behind the killings. I think, honestly, that these bastards are just a little too greedy."

★

Chapter 17

Dawn came slowly, gray against the windowpane and gray in the streets beyond, then, finally, revealing a cloudless blue sky.

Jessie, sleeping in a large chair trimmed with gold leaf, and with her slim finger wrapped lightly around the trigger of the Colt in her lap, was the first to stir. She awoke, not to the familiar sound of birds, but to the rumbling of wagons and carriage wheels in the street.

For a long time, she gazed around the room, surveying its occupants with a careful eye, judging if anything was amiss. There was Stempley, asleep in the bed, above the covers. Curled on the opposite side, under the covers, was Amelia. On either side of the bed, in two chairs, were Ki and Stratton. The captain slept with a shotgun cradled in his lap. Ki's hands were empty, but they in themselves were worth more than Stratton's scattergun.

"Good morning," Ki said, his voice a soft whisper.

So, Jessie was not the first to awaken. Ki was awake also, or had just opened his eyes ever so little. Jessie wondered if he had not slept the entire night, or perhaps he was awakened by whatever slight stirring she had made when she awoke.

"Ah, morning already, is it?" Stratton yawned, then stretched, drawn from a sound sleep by Ki's greeting.

Next came Stempley, stretching out full on the bed, even before opening his eyes. "I see we've all survived the night," he said, when he finally did open his eyes.

Amelia remained sleeping, curling herself into a small ball at the sound of the voices.

Jessie rose, stretched, and holstered the pistol.

Stratton was just rising, too, when there was a soft knock at the door. Instinctively, his hands gripped the shotgun tighter, his finger searching out the trigger.

Motioning Stempley to silence, Jessie rose, crossed the room, and quickly took her gun out of the holster before she opened the door.

Raising the gun at head level, she clicked back the hammer as Stratton raised the shotgun.

There, an expression of fear and surprise spread across his face, was a waiter, wheeling in a cart that held coffee, tea, a large plate of fruit, and another plate that contained toast and rolls.

"Would you folks want me to come back later?" he asked, breathless with fear.

"No, that's fine," Stratton said, lowering the shotgun. "Just wheel it in anywhere."

The waiter surveyed the scene of Jessie with her Colt, now held at her side, Stratton with his shotgun, and Amelia sleeping in bed next to a fully clothed Stempley. "I can come back, if that's more suited to you," he said.

"Now's as good a time as any," Jessie said.

"Yes ma'am, I imagine it is," the waiter answered, abandoning the cart and turning to leave.

"Wait!" Stratton called.

The waiter immediately froze, afraid of what fresh oddity was to come, perhaps even his own death at the hands of one of these lunatics.

Stratton stepped forward, shotgun down at his side and handed the waiter a coin. "Sorry for the inconvenience," he said.

"No inconvenience, none at all sir," the waiter replied, looking down at the coin as if it were some strange rock he'd just discovered.

"And we'd appreciate it if you didn't mention any of this," Stratton said, motioning around the room with a casual wave of the shotgun.

"No sir," the waiter replied numbly.

"My uncle and his niece, they are quite wary of the city," Stratton said. "Unusual as it seems, they fear for their personal safety."

"I understand. The city can be frightening, a frightening place," the waiter replied. "May I leave now, sir?"

"Of course," Stratton said.

Just to be certain, the frightened waiter looked to Jessie, who offered a wan smile. Then he was gone, heading quickly out the door.

"I should have said something, I suppose," Stempley said. "I've given instructions to the kitchen to have my breakfast sent up every morning at this time. Usually the waiter uses a passkey."

Jessie shuddered to think what might have happened had the waiter just opened the door without knocking.

Stratton by now had begun drinking a cup of coffee, while Amelia stirred, slowly stretching like a cat before opening her eyes.

They ate breakfast in silence, all of them lost in thoughts about what the day would bring. As far as Jessie saw, it was just a matter of stalling Stempley long enough for them to flush the bastards out in the open. But that meant that it was also a matter of keeping his greed under control as well. If Stempley's greed and fear, those twin driving forces of every businessman, could be harnessed and held back for just a little while longer, they might have a chance of figuring out who was behind the murders.

Just as they were finishing, there was another knock at the door. Jessie moved toward it, but saw that it was neither a waiter nor a visitor. Someone had slipped an envelope under the door. The envelope, which bore the name of the hotel in one corner, was addressed to Stempley.

Jessie retrieved it and handed it to him as he walked back into the room wearing a fresh suit.

"Ah now, what could this be?" he asked, tearing the envelope open. From inside he extracted a yellow sheet of paper, which Jessie immediately recognized as the type that bore telegraph messages.

"What does it say?" Stratton asked, moving toward Stempley, anxious to hear any news.

Stempley studied it for a long time, his face pulling down into a frown as he reread the words. "The bank's representative will be here this afternoon," he said, his voice grim.

"Anything else?" Jessie asked.

"It seems that because of the last death, the bank has lowered the price it is willing to offer for my stock shares."

"Those thieving bastards!" Stratton spat.

"They are offering not half, as they originally suggested," Stempley replied, "but now they are offering forty percent."

"Surely you couldn't entertain such an offer," Jessie said. "You might as well give the boat to them."

"But my dear, don't you see?" came the sad reply. "They all but own the ship already. The only reason they would possibly need my last shares is to make it official."

"Look, I don't give a damn if you didn't pay for the ship outright," Jessie said. "The fact of the matter is, it wouldn't have been built if it wasn't for you. I say that you hold on to your shares, until—"

"Until what?" Stempley replied angrily. "Until I'm as dead as Moran and the others?"

It wasn't until then that it hit Jessie. The question seemed so obvious, she was surprised that she didn't ask it before. "Why aren't you dead?" she asked.

"I beg your pardon," Stempley answered, more than a little peeved.

"I asked why you're not dead like the others," Jessie repeated. "Let's suppose it is the bank behind the killings, no matter how they're doing them. Why don't they just kill you as they did the others?"

"Yes, why didn't they kill you?" Stratton asked, moving closer. "You'd be the first one I'd kill. The most likely choice."

"I beg your pardon," Stempley repeated, his voice now filled with outrage.

"You are the oldest among the investors," Jessie said. "You would be the most likely target."

"Why are they even making the offer to buy the stocks?" Stratton added. "Why not just kill you like they did the others?"

Stratton sat down on the edge of the bed, his eyes going from Jessie to Ki, and then back again. "Because I don't own the stocks," he said.

"You don't own them?" Jessie asked.

"I do, in a manner of speaking," he said. "But on paper I don't. It's a very complex business arrangement, which I don't think you'd rather hear."

"Oh, I think I'd rather hear it," Stratton said, moving closer to the old man. There was more than a touch of menace in his walk. "If I'm going to risk my life for something, I want to hear all about it."

"It's very complicated," Stempley said. "But it

boils down to this. The other investors were much younger than me, very much younger. There were certain concessions made, because of my age. It was, naturally enough, assumed that I would be the first of the group to pass on."

"So you'd never see the full profit from your investment," Jessie said. "Is that what was worrying you? You were afraid you'd die of old age before the ship turned a profit."

"In a word, yes," Stempley confessed. "It was important that I see the profits before the others, or at least a greater share of them in the beginning. I was allowed to hold twice the number of stock shares as the others. I was the majority stockholder, if you must know, though with the same voting power. It was agreed, from the start."

"But if you held more stocks, then you'd have more votes," Jessie said. "That's the way it works."

"No, we arranged my stocks differently," came the reply. "If I died, half of my shares would be returned to the bank. But the other shares, they were never in my name. I never owned them."

"Then who owned them?" Amelia asked suddenly.

"A company owns them," Stempley explained. "And I own half a share in that company, which is a meat processing plant."

"Who owns the other half of the company?" Stratton asked, but he already knew the answer.

"The bank, of course," Stempley said. "It was a very neat arrangement. I own the stocks, but can't vote them. At the same time, the bank can't vote them, either. On the other hand, if I chose to sell my stocks, the bank would own everything."

"But if you died?" Jessie asked.

"Then my heirs, whoever I put in my will, would own those shares as well as the meat packing company," Stempley said. "As I mentioned, it's all very complicated."

"But it comes down to the bank having to buy those shares," Jessie said. "They must buy them to keep control of the ship. Killing you gets them nothing."

"That's right," Stempley replied. "They need me alive to sell them the shares. The other men thought they would live forever, so the shares were in their names. The fools. They should have known better."

"So, what do you intend to do?" Stratton asked.

Stempley frowned. "I've thought of it the entire night, and I've come to a conclusion. I intend to sell them the ship," he said. "If they want it so badly, then they can have it, and by heavens, I hope they choke on it. I'll wash my hands of the whole filthy mess."

"What a coward you are," Jessie said disgustedly. "What a filthy, greedy coward you are."

"It's a business decision, nothing more," the old man replied.

"What about your friends?" Stratton asked. "What about all those poor dead sons of bitches?"

"They were businessmen," Stempley said. "Do you think they would show me any loyalty in my grave? Hell, they even expected me to die first. Wherever they are, I'm sure they understand. It isn't anything personal, just business."

"You know, all my life I've listened to rich bastards say that," Stratton said. "They always say, 'It's not personal, just business.' And the one thing I've learned, the minute you hear one of them say it, you better run. You better run just as fast as you can, because that so-called business decision is gonna be just as personal as hell to you or somebody else."

★

Chapter 18

Jessie, seeing no reason to guard Stempley any further, stayed in the room with Ki, Stratton, and Amelia to decide what to do next. Stempley, for his part, departed the room with as much dignity as he could muster, which wasn't much.

"I say we just leave, Ki," Jessie suggested. "I'm all for getting on that train, heading back for Texas, and leaving that bastard to his own damn devices."

"Just like that?" Amelia said. "What about me?"

"What about you?" Jessie answered, a little baffled by the young woman's question.

"You think I'll still have a job once the bankers get their hands on that ship?" she answered.

"I could say the same thing," Stratton put in. "I'd quit; I'm ready to quit, but more than likely those bankers will get some youngster to captain their damned ship. Either that, or they'll cut the salary in half."

"Thirty people work on that ship, Miss Starbuck," Amelia said. "They'll cut all their pay. Those bankers will cut their pay and fire half of them."

"I've seen that happen before," Stratton added. "Forget about me—what about all those other people? Are you just gonna run out on them?"

"I don't see what I can do," Jessie answered. "Stempley isn't the same man my father knew and that I knew a long time ago. He's changed."

"Perhaps he has not changed," Ki offered.

"Oh, he's changed all right, Ki," Jessie answered. "The Stempley I knew wouldn't let a bunch of bankers and such scare him."

"Men sometimes, they live their lives asleep," Ki mused. "They become tired and fall asleep. They work and sleep and eat, but they are not awake. Perhaps we need only to wake him."

"What in hell are you talking about?" Stratton asked. "He ain't asleep, he's awake as anyone I ever saw. Got his eyes open wide."

"Perhaps, and then perhaps not," Ki replied. "Tell me, why would an old man prize money above friendship and above lives? Because he is a man asleep, he has forgotten how to live and how to fight."

"Suppose he is asleep, as you say," came Stratton's response. "How do you know he's gonna wake up soon? Or for that matter, what's gonna wake him up?"

"Mr. Stempley—he was a brave man once," Ki said. "I feel if we show him who to fight, he will wake up."

"Ki, it sounds real nice, but he knows who to fight," Jessie broke in. "It's the damn bankers. I don't know who specifically, but it's those bankers."

"We must show him who," Ki said.

"Well, I don't know about you people, but I'm going to go out and see what I can come up with," Stratton said, then headed for the door.

The others, unsure of what course of action to take, followed him out. As it happened, they did not have to journey far. No sooner had they reached the bottom of the stairs that led into the lobby than they were stopped by a sight that brought them up short.

There, standing in the center of the lobby, smoking a cigar, was Quigley, the drowned investor.

"Do you see what I see?" Jessie asked, turning numbly toward Stratton.

"I see it, but I don't believe it," the captain said. "It doesn't make any sense."

A moment later, Quigley turned slowly around and spotted the four on the stairs. A broad smile came to his face and he rushed forward. "My dear captain, Jessie, and why, it's Amelia, isn't it?" he asked, embracing first Stratton, then Jessie.

"I don't understand," Jessie stammered. "What happened? We thought you drowned."

"Drowned? Nonsense!" Quigley beamed. "Just because I fell overboard in the middle of the night? Ha!"

"But we thought—" Stratton began.

Quigley's smile grew a shade larger. "I'll toy with you no more, dear captain," he said. "Fall over into the river I did. The moment I felt the icy embrace of the river, I thought myself a dead man. Then, by heavens, I began to swim."

"Swim?" Jessie asked, disbelieving.

"Yes, by heavens, swim!" Quigley announced. "I swam with the current, letting it carry me downriver a half mile or so before I caught a piece of debris, a large log."

"You held on to a log?" Amelia asked, breathless with the details of the story and the heroics.

"Held on for dear life, my dear girl," Quigley said. "Held on and let it carry me farther downriver. By dawn, exhausted and nearly out of my mind, I managed to make my way to shore. There, I wandered inland, I don't know how far. Shoeless, my suit torn to shreds, drenched, and exhausted, I was discovered at last by a farmer."

"A remarkable story," Jessie said.

"Ah, but it's not over," Quigley continued. "At first the poor man didn't believe I was who I said I was. Frankly, in my state, I don't blame him, not at all. However, he took pity on me and my wretched condition just the same. He loaned me a suit of his meager clothes, and two days later he provided a carriage by which we found the local sheriff. It was only a matter of time and telegraph, and here I stand before you."

"I've never heard of such a thing!" Amelia said, awed.

"Neither have I," Quigley agreed. "But tell me, what is the news? The ship, from which I've just returned, is nearly without a crew. Where are the others? Where are my fellows in good fortune?"

"It's a long story," Jessie said.

"Time—I have nothing but time," Quigley countered.

"I'm afraid you have precious little time," Stratton answered.

Quigley smiled, put one arm around Stratton and the other around Jessie, and led them off to the hotel bar. "Then come, we shall have a drink and you shall tell me the story in all due haste."

It didn't take long before Quigley, sitting behind a large brandy, altered his mood. His face changed slowly from merriment to sorrow as Jessie and Stratton recounted the circumstances surrounding the death of each of his friends. When they reached the part about the bankers, his face grew bright red with rage. His hands shook and he cursed. "Oh, those bastards," he said. "I felt myself pushed, but couldn't be certain. Oh, those bastards won't get away with it! Where is Stempley now? Where is that lowly coward?"

"He's probably in the hotel library," Jessie said. "He's probably meeting the banker now."

"Then let's be off," Quigley announced, "and put an end to this travesty!"

They followed the little businessman out of the hotel saloon and through the lobby. The library was at the back of the hotel, adjoining the lobby. Its walls were lined with books and portraits of the city. A dozen or more large leather chairs and a few tables were positioned so that guests could read in comfort. Sitting in one corner were

Stempley and a gray little fat man.

"Cowards! Fools! Murderers! Bankers!" Quigley screamed as he entered the large room.

Stempley looked up from the papers, his face a mask of disbelief. "Duncan!" he shouted, starting to rise.

"Away from me!" Quigley shouted, dismissing Stempley with a wave of his hand. "You disgust me!"

The small little gray man began to rise, but before he could, Quigley grabbed a walking stick from one of the other guests and began to beat him.

Blow after blow landed across the little man's back until he was cowering, then running. "Please, Mr. Quigley, this is no way—no way at all to do business!" the little man howled as he bent under the blows of the cane.

Quigley followed the man out, still bringing the walking stick down across his back until they reached the door. When they had progressed as far as the large threshold, Quigley gave the banker a swift kick to the back of his pants, sending him sailing into the lobby facefirst.

Jessie, Ki, Stratton, Amelia, and Stempley watched, amazed, as Quigley ran back to the desk, hurriedly jammed the papers that were there into the banker's satchel, then ran to the door and hurled them out into the lobby.

"Bravo!" Stratton called.

Jessie, smiling, watched as Quigley, panting, approached. "And that's how I like to see my bankers—whipped like dogs," he said. "Whipped like dogs."

"But, I don't understand," Stempley began. "I thought—"

"I know damn well what you thought," Quigley said. "You thought of nothing but yourself."

"But I thought you were—"

"What was he offering you? Tell me!" Quigley demanded. "Seventy-five cents on the dollar?"

Stempley didn't answer.

"What was it? Sixty? You fool, you'd accept sixty?"

Stempley shook his head.

"Less?" Quigley shouted, outraged. "I should be at you worse than he. At least he wasn't a fool. What was it? Fifty cents on the dollar?"

"Forty," Stempley said in a near whisper. "But you have to understand—"

"I understand. I understand perfectly," Quigley said. "I understand that I took on a fool as a partner. A complete and utter fool."

"You have to understand, I thought you were dead," Stempley said lamely.

"I understand that such a fool has no business owning such a beautiful ship," Quigley said, raising the walking stick as if to hit Stempley. "Any man who would sell his shares for forty cents on the dollar to bankers has no business, no right owning such a beautiful thing."

"I owe you an apology," Stempley said at last.

"Damn your apologies," Quigley replied. "Damn you and your apologies. I can't bear to look at you."

"But I thought—"

"I know. You thought I was dead," Quigley mimicked. Then quickly changed his tone to say, "You would accept forty from a damned banker, then you damn well better accept fifty from me."

"But now that you're alive—" Stempley tried.

"Now that I'm alive, I don't want anything to do with you," Quigley countered. "Do you accept my offer?"

"I don't or can't see where you leave me any choice," Stempley said.

"No choice at all, you coward," Quigley replied. "I'll have my lawyers bring the papers over this very evening."

The others watched the entire transaction with some shock, but also with satisfaction. "Bravo!" Stratton said as Quigley turned from the room.

As soon as Quigley heard the captain's exclamation, he turned, "And, as for you, my dear captain, don't think that your loyalty will go unrepaid," he said. "Not at all. I remember my friends. And that goes for all of you."

Then they all watched as he vanished out the door, pausing just long enough to return the walking stick to its owner.

Stempley, when he was certain that Quigley had left the lobby, raised himself tiredly from the chair and followed him out without saying a word to anyone.

"Well, I guess that settles it," Stratton said. "Now we at least know the ship is in good hands. It'll take a man like Quigley to stand up to the bankers. I wouldn't be surprised if he managed to buy out their shares with his own money."

"He seemed mad enough to do it," Jessie said.

"Mad enough to buy the damned bank," Stratton answered. "And rich enough, too."

★
Chapter 19

Hours later, Jessie was dressing in her room. Somehow, someone had arranged for Stempley's shares in the ship to be signed over to Quigley in a formal ceremony in the dining room. In just a few minutes everything would be put right, and she could return to Texas, where she belonged.

Just as she was getting ready to leave, there was a soft knock on the door. Thinking it was a waiter or some such, she crossed the room and opened the door.

Standing there, wearing a dapper suit, was Givens. "Surprised?" he asked.

"No more than usual," she said, ushering him into the room. "But you're too late. It's all finished."

"What? What's finished?" the gambler asked.

"Everything," Jessie answered. "Quigley wasn't drowned after all. Now he's buying Stempley's shares in the ship. And he's promised a full and thorough investigation into the murders. He said he won't rest until the criminals are brought to justice."

"What? That's impossible," Givens gasped.

"What's so impossible?" Jessie said. "That there's at least one honest businessman in the world?"

"That in itself is impossible," Givens noted. "But you should read this!"

Jessie took the newspaper clipping that Givens pulled from his pocket and read it with increasing horror, her eyes widening after each line.

"And you would malign my noble and honest profession," Givens said with an air of some self-satisfaction.

"We have to stop them!" Jessie nearly screamed. "And we have to stop them now!"

"Where are they?"

"All of them, the crew, everyone, they're down in the ballroom!"

Without another word, they dashed out the door and headed for the ballroom at a full run. Jessie was grateful that she had abandoned the idea of wearing a fancy dress in favor of her usual attire. She was even more grateful that she had strapped her Colt on just before Givens arrived.

In the ballroom, Jessie found the entire crew of the ship, Stratton, Amelia, and Ki watching, as up on the dais, Quigley was just then handing a thick pile of papers over to Stempley to sign. She knew that the papers, once signed, would hand the entire ship over to Quigley.

"No!" Jessie shouted from the ballroom entrance. "Don't do it!"

Every eye in the large room turned on Jessie as she stood in the door. The only face that didn't look panicked or confused was that of Quigley. "Miss Starbuck, fear not, we wouldn't dream of finalizing this deal without you," he said smoothly.

A small ripple of laughter drifted through the audience at the small joke.

"Don't do it, Stempley, it's a trick! The whole thing is a trick!"

"Jessie, are you insane?" Stratton hissed. "Get the hell out of here if you can't be quiet."

"No," Jessie said, pulling the newspaper clipping from her pocket. "Look at this!"

"Listen to her!" Givens said. "She's right!"

Stratton grabbed the newspaper clipping hurriedly and began to read. Almost immediately his face turned to one of rage. "Quigley, you damned bastard!" he yelled.

"What is it?" Quigley asked. "What is it you have there?"

"It's a wedding announcement. From a St. Louis newspaper," Jessie said. "It's the announcement of Quigley's daughter marrying Doctor Wittick!"

The audience sat there stunned, no one knowing what to make of the news.

"Wittick's family owns the bank!" Jessie proclaimed. "He's a banker's son! Quigley will own the ship with the bank. He'll practically own the bank."

"Is that true?" Stempley asked, turning to Quigley. "You arranged for those killings?"

"I deny everything, everything," Quigley said.

"It makes sense," Jessie shouted loudly. "Wittick did the killings. All of them!"

As if to offer positive proof of his guilt, Wittick bolted, charging out of the ballroom as fast as he could.

"Get him!" a voice cried from the crowd.

"Kill that son of a banker!"

A moment later, the crew rose as one and took off after the young man, chasing him from the hotel.

"The fool, the young fool," Quigley mumbled. "Never run. Always deny. Deny. Deny. Deny."

"Is it true?" Stempley asked Quigley. "You son of a bitch, is it true?"

"What does it matter, you old fool?" came the answer. "What in hell does it matter now?"

It still mattered to Stempley. Faster than even he could have suspected he could move, Stempley had his hands around Quigley's throat, choking the life out of him.

"I know where Wittick is heading," Stratton said. "He must be heading back to the boat."

Givens rushed the stage and positioned himself behind Stempley, trying to pry his hands free. "Don't, don't," he whispered in the old man's ear. "There's no percentage in it."

As Jessie and Stratton left the ballroom, Givens managed to pry Stempley off Quigley and quiet the older man down.

Jessie and Stratton reached the street at a run and turned toward the docks. "How do you know he's on the ship?" she asked, panting with the run.

"Has to be," Stratton answered. "Searching for a last bit of evidence against him. Besides, it's the last place they'll look for him."

When they reached the ship, the salon was darkened. Jessie drew her gun as Stratton lit a match and touched it to the wick of a lamp.

Suddenly a shot rang out, the bullet whizzing by Jessie's head as the muzzle flash illuminated a shadow at the other end of the salon.

Jessie returned fire and ran toward the place where she'd seen the shadow.

As Stratton raised the lamp, she clearly saw the door that led into the hall.

Jessie peered around the door cautiously as Stratton came up next to her with the lamp. "He must be heading for his cabin," he said.

Her Colt out, Jessie eased her way into the darkened corridor. Stratton, right behind her, lighted the way with the lamp.

When they were halfway down the hall, a door flew open and Wittick kicked out, knocking the lamp from Stratton's hand, breaking its base and chimney. Blue-and-yellow flame washed over the floor and up the walls. A second later, Jessie was blinded by a punch to the head.

She raised the Colt and fired, but Wittick was already turning the corner. "Get the fire out!" she instructed Stratton, but saw it was already futile.

A second later, she was taking off down the hall after Wittick.

Following the narrow stairs down, she found herself in the darkened kitchen. Another shot split the darkness, the bullet clanging off a pot as the door at the far end of the room slammed shut.

Jessie approached the door cautiously. "Wittick, there's no place to go!" she said. "Where can you hide?"

Footsteps sounded below her and she followed them down. Above her, a bell was ringing. Suddenly she could smell smoke. It must have been Stratton, summoning help because the fire was out of control.

At the foot of the stairs she found herself in the engine room. Piles of cordwood were stacked everywhere.

"Wittick, the ship's on fire," she called.

Someone moved at the other side of the room. There was a mumbled voice and then another shot rang out.

Sticking close to the wood, she inched her way forward. And there was Wittick standing in front of the boiler, pistol drawn. At his feet was the body of the boiler tender. "It's hot, Miss Starbuck," Wittick said, sweat pouring down his face. "If you miss, you could blow the ship up with both of us on it."

"You can't get away with this," Jessie said, moving slowly forward.

"But I already have," he said. "I've nearly already gotten away with it. Now put the gun down."

"Where are you going to go?" Jessie asked. "Think about it. You're a rich man's son. Where can you hide?"

"Europe, France, it doesn't matter," Wittick said. "Remember, I'm a doctor. There's always a job for a doctor."

"A lot of people seem to die around you, for being a doctor," Jessie said, taking a step closer.

"You don't have to be a good one," came the answer. "Now put the gun down."

"No," Jessie said. "You're coming back up with me."

"You leave me no choice, then," Wittick answered, and raised the gun to take aim.

But Jessie beat him to the draw, firing first. The bullet hit him square in the throat, shattering his spinal cord and continuing on to lodge itself in the boiler. The impact spun the young man around as the boiler's side ripped open. A thick burst of steam caught him full in the face for a moment before he dropped.

Jessie stood there stunned, then heard the ripping metal as the boiler burst. Turning, she ran back up the stairs as the explosion surged through the engine room, covering her in steam. She ran back through the kitchen, running from steam to smoke as the boiler rumbled again, then ripped a huge hole in the hull.

When she reached the cabin hall, it was covered in flames. Backtracking, she found the stairs up to the salon, which was also filled with flames. Running blindly through the flame, she managed to reach the door and then the deck. As the ship

179

listed heavily toward the dock, she ran up the gangplank. Only when she had reached the dock did she look back. The entire riverboat was covered in fire, every window illuminated with bright flames.

"That's just one hell of a thing," a familiar voice at her side said.

Turning to face Stratton, she saw that he was covered in black soot. The arms and legs of his clothing were singed from fighting the fire. "There goes your ship," she said.

"You know what they say about ships, don't you?" Stratton asked, looking straight into her beautiful face, now lit by the flames from the burning ship.

"That they're holes in the water where fools throw their money?" Jessie answered, the heat forcing her to take several steps back.

"Exactly," Stratton answered.

A special offer for people who enjoy reading the best Westerns published today.

WESTERNS!

NO OBLIGATION

Mail the coupon below

To start your subscription and receive 2 FREE WESTERNS, fill out the coupon below and mail it today. We'll send your first shipment which includes 2 FREE BOOKS as soon as we receive it.

Mail To: **True Value Home Subscription Services, Inc. P.O. Box 5235**
120 Brighton Road, Clifton, New Jersey 07015-5235

YES! I want to start reviewing the very best Westerns being published today. Send me my first shipment of 6 Westerns for me to preview FREE for 10 days. If I decide to keep them, I'll pay for just 4 of the books at the low subscriber price of $2.75 each; a total $11.00 (a $21.00 value). Then each month I'll receive the 6 newest and best Westerns to preview Free for 10 days. If I'm not satisfied I may return them within 10 days and owe nothing. Otherwise I'll be billed at the special low subscriber rate of $2.75 each; a total of $16.50 (at least a $21.00 value) and save $4.50 off the publishers price. There are never any shipping, handling or other hidden charges. I understand I am under no obligation to purchase any number of books and I can cancel my subscription at any time, no questions asked. In any case the 2 FREE books are mine to keep.

Name _____

Street Address _____ Apt. No. _____

City _____ State _____ Zip Code _____

Telephone _____

Signature _____
(if under 18 parent or guardian must sign)

Terms and prices subject to change. Orders subject
to acceptance by True Value Home Subscription
Services, Inc.

11455-3